HAMSTER GANGSTER

HAMSTER
GANGSTER

Angela Robb

Matador
9 Priory Business Park,
Wistow Road, Kibworth Beauchamp,
Leicestershire. LE8 0RX
Tel: 0116 279 2299
Email: books@troubador.co.uk
Web: www.troubador.co.uk/matador
Twitter: @matadorbooks

ISBN 978 1789016 710

British Library Cataloguing in Publication Data.
A catalogue record for this book is available from the British Library.

Printed on FSC accredited paper
Printed and bound in Great Britain by 4edge Limited
Typeset in 12pt Book Antiqua by Troubador Publishing Ltd, Leicester, UK

Matador is an imprint of Troubador Publishing Ltd

For all the pocket-money pets

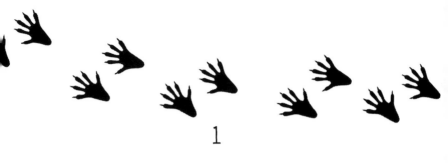

1

An Ingenious Plan

I have been hiding under my sawdust for long enough to be sure: the Fiend is safely out of the house, at a meeting of the Junior Jungle Scouts.

So let me fill you in while the coast is clear.

My problem is this: ten days ago I arrived in the home of the most dangerous mini-human in the world. He is four feet high, with beady eyes and an evil smile that shows off his sticky-out teeth. He is utterly nutty, and deadly violent. His name is Gary Bickle.

Too many times have I been grabbed and squeezed and thrown, and kicked around the carpet in a plastic ball – all at the hands of this bully. But one thing is for certain: my days of living with the villain Gary will be short-lived. It is time to stand up for myself. After all, I am nearly eight weeks old.

1

But before I carry out my clever plan, or begin to think of one, I had better introduce myself. My name is Rocco the Fantastic. Or it would have been, had my mother had time to think of it before I was whisked away from her at an early age. As it happens, she only got as far as 'Rocco', so you may call me just that. As I am a hamster, you might think that I am very small. This is not the case. In fact, I am particularly large when compared with a great many creatures, such as grasshoppers, and baby mice.

Now, even as I was telling you that, another compartment in my brain was already planning my escape from Gary's lair. I have now reviewed this plan, and I think you will agree that it is genius. It is a two-step strategy:

Step 1: Be in plastic hamster ball.
Step 2: Exit house.

A few details are missing because some things cannot be planned or predicted: one must respond to the circumstances as they unfold. Of course, the circumstances will involve the Enemy himself, as well as Pesky and Ginger.

I have not yet told you about Pesky and Ginger. The first is a tall, skinny, wild-eyed fellow whose tongue always hangs out the left side of his mouth. He is a hound of some kind, and an idiot of every kind. He is very friendly and playful – in other words, extremely dangerous from a hamster's point of view. But Ginger is a cat, and she is crafty and determined, which makes her the worst foe of all. It is fortunate, then, that I am smarter than she.

Once I am past them, I have one vital tool in my survivalist's toolkit. You see, we hamsters are equipped with spacious pouches in our cheeks for carrying essential supplies. Right now, my cheeks are positively bulging. I have been careful to pack only the most nutritious foodstuffs, including hamster muesli and choc drops.

My extraordinary sense of hearing tells me that the car has just pulled into the driveway. So, Gary Bickle, you return from Junior Jungle Scouts.

My plan, like my food supplies, is safely tucked away inside my head. The time is near.

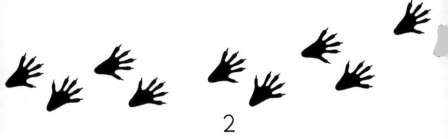

2

The Not-So-Great Escape

One moment – please.

Wait till … I catch my breath … and I'll tell you everything that just happened …

Okay, so … On entering the house, the Menace came straight to his bedroom. He played his favourite video game for eight minutes, until his attention span was used up. Then he approached my cage. *Perfect*.

'ROCCO!' he shouted. 'COME OUT AND PLAY!'

He reached in, grabbed me. He dropped me into the familiar plastic ball, screwed it shut …

And let it go.

I left my stomach far behind as the hamster ball plummeted. Gary caught it on top of his foot, and kicked it upwards, over and over again.

I clamped both hands over my mouth to stop myself being sick.

At last, he grabbed the ball and shook it – and my efforts not to be sick came to an unfortunate end. Then, finally, he put me down – *on top of his desk*.

'HA-HA-HA-HA-HA!'

The unexpected, just as expected, was happening. So, you are probably asking, what does this fantastic hamster do now? Here is *exactly* what I do.

I roll across the desk, looking for a suitable way down, knocking twelve-inch Octo-Man *and* the Amazing Beetleboy out of my way. There is no suitable way down.

So I drop. I spin. I bounce. I tear across the carpet, weaving my way between countless toys. I come to a paper map of the world. I cross continents, and oceans littered with little grey battleships. Then I hear fighter planes, diving and firing overhead. It is Gary, armed with a plastic jet.

I am hit! (by his foot). The world tumbles, but I recover quickly and roll under the bed. And what do I find? An army of green soldiers! Their intentions are unclear, but I trust no one, so I bowl them over anyway. Then it's back out into the light – except at that very moment Gary drops his duvet on me.

'BLACKOUT!' he yells.

No matter. Rolling in any direction will get me out, so I begin to move. But then I hesitate – this could be my chance to sneak out of the room unnoticed. I wait for a minute. *Bingo.* The sound of explosions tells me that You-Know-Who has returned to his video game. So I bowl silently to the edge of the duvet, and make for the door.

I'm out of the bedroom, simple as that. Now you might think the steep staircase would be scary – but not for me, a fearless survival expert. I bounce from one stair to the next and fly straight into the kitchen.

That's where it all kicks off. Ginger streaks in through the cat flap, straight past Gary's mum, who is mopping the floor. She springs on the ball, sticks her claws in the air holes, and *pulls.* I run as hard as I can, but her grip is too tight. A gap opens around the middle of the ball. A dainty pink nose forces its way through. In a flash, I seize this dainty pink nose in my jaws. With a yowl Ginger drops the ball, and I roll back along the hall.

So what next, you ask? Surely the cat will be back, madder than ever?

Spot on.

Lucky, then, that in five seconds flat I steer my way into the living room and enlist my secret weapon. That is, I accidentally activate my secret weapon by rolling over his back paw, just as

6

Ginger bursts into the room. Pesky springs to his feet and starts to yap. With a screech, Ginger turns and flees.

Pesky is a handful, but I know what to do. I curl myself up tight as the ball spins. I can feel the dog's hot breath, steaming up the plastic. I feel dizzy – but I know that a brainwave is near.

Pesky nudges me under the coffee table. Here I show how clever I can be without even trying, because I come to a stop right next to a chunk of chocolate chip cookie. As Pesky squeezes himself under the table in a bid for the biscuit, I roll out of the room.

And so back to the kitchen. The mop is propped against the sink, next to the back door. Which, as I already mentioned, has a cat flap. So here's what I do.

I roll up to the mop and knock it over. It lies in front of the door. I move into position, take a run at it, strike the handle. I'm tossed over it, landing right by the back door, under the cat flap.

I need to build up more speed.

I roll back out of the kitchen and along the hall. Gary's mum heads for the stairs with her laundry basket and starts to climb. I turn and bowl fast along the hallway. In the kitchen, the phone starts to ring. Gary's mum thuds back down the stairs, unaware of my approach, and at the foot of the stairs, we meet.

She kicks me, hard, into the kitchen. The world spins. I hit the mop handle, fly, smack into the cat flap, get blinded by daylight, bounce – and stop. It is a perfect escape.

The only slight difficulty is that my ball is now wedged between the branches of a small dead bush. Of course, any minute now I will figure out a cunning way to free it. I just hope that I can do so before the Grey Streak reappears. Do not be alarmed, but this mysterious creature whizzed past more than once while I was telling of my adventure. What it is, I can't tell – but I sense that it has something to do with the loud cracking sounds coming from just behind the cherry blossom tree.

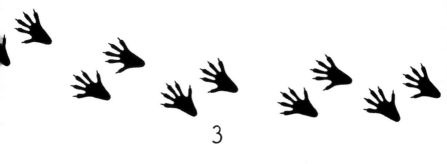

3

The Nutcracker

It is not because I am unable to free myself that I am still stuck in the small dead bush. It is because it is safest to remain here until the Grey Terror has gone away, as the tangle of branches ensures that I am rather well hidden. (It turns out, then, that what at first seemed like an unfortunate landing is actually the latest example of my genius.)

The rustling in the bush is not a good sign. What makes this new foe so dangerous is that it is completely unknown; without understanding its ways, it is much harder for me to plan its defeat.

'How very odd!'

Now that it is standing right in front of me, and talking, I can see that it has sharp front teeth and long, curling eyelashes. I can see it is a squirrel.

'A hamster in a plastic ball. What will they think of next?'

'*They* won't get the chance, because I have left *them* behind once and for all.'

'Is that so? Well, you'd better get out of their garden, then.'

She's altogether rude, but it's best to remain polite – for now.

'You're exactly right. So please step aside while I remove myself from this shrub, and I'll be on my way.'

'And just how *are* you going to remove yourself? And even if you do, what then? Are you to roll off into the sunset in your ball?'

She's not very smart, either: it won't be sunset for hours.

'Just watch and learn,' I tell her. 'And stand well *back* – please.'

Actually, I wish she would leave. For some reason I suddenly feel less sure of myself. She is watching me with her arms folded, which is very off-putting.

Running on the spot isn't working. I do not need the squirrel's raised eyebrow to tell me that. What else to try … How about ramming against the inside of the ball.

Ram the ball. That's it. Come on. Ram the ball.

Did you hear that? That was the squirrel, *sighing*.

'I heard that, you know,' I tell her.

'What did you hear?'

'You sighed. Don't say you didn't.'

'I won't say I didn't, because I did.'

'And why did you?'

'Because what you're doing is never going to work. Unless you're just trying to knock yourself silly. Or should I say sillier.'

This is too much.

'Go away.'

The look of pity on her face is the worst insult yet. This, and the fact that even as she's pulling on the branch underneath me, I can feel the ball start to move.

'Okay, hamster. Try running now.'

I slip gently on to the ground. I'm not going to thank her, if that's what she wants.

'A rather obvious way for you to speed up my escape. I wonder why you didn't think of it sooner.'

'Well, it was rather difficult to do while I was standing well back. Also, my sense of fun does get in the way. What's your name?'

'Rocco.' In my head I added 'the Fantastic', but somehow it didn't come out.

'My name is Sweet Pea.'

'Well I'm pleased to meet you.' Where did *that* come from?

'Likewise. Now, you'll be wanting out of that ball. I can help you there. Just let me show you something.' Off she goes. What could she possibly have, hidden behind that cherry blossom tree?

A large broken chestnut, apparently.

'One I did earlier. Trust me, this is a lot harder to crack than that plastic.' She's testing said plastic with her stupidly large teeth. 'Watch and learn,' she says with a sly smile.

I would of course think of some brilliantly witty reply, but she's already sinking her teeth into the ball.

And breaking a large hole in it.

'Come on out, then.'

'Actually I think I will.'

I have never felt grass beneath my feet before. It feels strange, and scratchy.

'So what are you going to do now, then?' asks Sweet Pea.

'I'm leaving, of course. I'm going to have adventures and be the hamster I was born to be.'

Now *both* her eyebrows are raised, which tells me she is curious, and impressed. 'And who exactly *is* the hamster you were born to be?'

That's it: the ultimate question. And I know I have the ultimate answer.

'I'll be the hamster who does just what he likes; the hamster who is bullied and thrown around by no one! I must lead other rodents into greatness. Just tell me: where do we live in the biggest numbers?'

'Well … if it's hordes of rodents you're looking for, you want to head for the Big City.'

It sounds so magical I have to say it back. 'The *Big City*.'

'But I wouldn't recommend it. These aren't friendly rodents. In fact, from what I've heard, they're ruthless criminals who won't be *led* by a pet hamster.'

This is fascinating. I need to hear more, but first I must correct the squirrel on one point:

'I'm not a pet hamster any more.'

'Good luck explaining that to *them*. I'm talking about huge gangs of murderous rats, Rocco. Besides, they're not the only ones you have to worry about. There are foxes, magpies, stray cats and dogs …'

'Ah-ha! Then it's just as well that cats and dogs are a speciality of mine. I happen to have plenty of experience defeating them.'

Sweet Pea hesitates. I can tell that she is finally starting to realise I am a force to be reckoned with.

'Then there are the humans,' she says.

Humans! As if I've never come across *those* before.

'Lots and lots of humans. At war with everything else that moves. Trust me: in the city, if you're not their pet, they want you dead.'

'Then it's fortunate indeed that I have already outsmarted the very worst of them.'

There's that sigh again. I think Sweet Pea has figured out that it's pointless to argue against my superior good sense.

'Did I mention,' she says weakly, 'that the city is dirty, and smelly, and loud?'

'Tell me this: have you ever been stuck in a cage that hasn't been cleaned out for a week, in a room with a small boy firing heavy artillery?'

'I have no idea what you're talking about.'

'I didn't think so. Now, can you please tell me how to get to the Big City?'

'Of course.' She scurries up the cherry blossom tree. I can see her perched among its lower branches. She is pointing ... north. Or possibly south. 'The city's over there. You can see the taller buildings from up here.'

'Very good.' I don't need to waste effort on climbing a tree; I'll be seeing those buildings up close soon enough. Sweet Pea is demonstrating that she can also climb *down* a tree head first. If that sounds impressive, it really isn't.

'So,' she says, 'how are you going to get there?'

'I don't know yet. Feats of brilliance must often be spontaneous.'

'I see. Well I suppose there's nothing left to say, except good luck.'

'Thank you. You've been most helpful.' I mean

by telling me about the Big City. Not by spoiling my chance to display my skills in plastic ball smashing.

And so we part company. There's not a moment to lose, so it's straight round to the front of the house. This brings me beneath the open window of Evil Boy's bedroom. His yelling is very loud, as is his mum's on the subject of responsible pet ownership. Clearly, they are aware of my disappearance.

It's time to hit the city. And yep – you guessed it – I think I just found the way.

4

Hang on a Minute...

There are two choices. The first is a van, City Slick Removals Ltd, parked outside the house opposite. I suspect it might stay there for quite some time, so I believe I'll go with option number two: the Crash Course School of Motoring, currently braked to a halt in the centre of the road. Clearly, the person driving this car is taking a course of professional training. And you can see the difference that makes. They appear to be turning the car around in no less than twelve separate stages – a complicated manoeuvre indeed.

All I have to do is grab on. Of course, I have to be careful as I hurry across the front lawn; don't forget I'm right under Gary's window. The shouting in his room has stopped. Is that worrying?

Yes, it is. A sudden burst of gunfire, and I make a dash for the flower border. I lay low beneath the pansies. But fear not: Gary has merely returned to his video game, and is firing at someone else. This gives me eight minutes to make myself scarce.

The trainee professional is still hard at work, easing the car backwards. With a burst of speed, they drive it up over the kerb and into a post. A curious thing to do, since the number plate is now hanging from the back of the car at an odd angle; but I suppose a real driver must learn to perform such advanced techniques, and a first attempt may be slightly flawed.

Anyway, this is altogether helpful. So without further ado, it's straight through the fence, across the pavement and on to the road. The car has turned around now, and is sitting still again. With a good ... running ... *jump* ... I take hold of the hanging edge of the number plate. Now all I have to do is hang on.

I'm ready and waiting. *Go on – give it some revs!* Or – okay then – quite a few revs ... And we're off!

We're building speed ... I can feel a warm breeze rushing through my fur. It is absolutely –

Whoa! I guess that's how we take a corner! I'm still holding on, and I'm learning to move with the forces: swing my body this way ... swing my body that way ...

Ow. The tyres just threw up a stone. I suppose that can't be avoided, but – ahh! – *please try!* That one struck me in the stomach. My eyes are watering, my fingers slipping – just a little. We whirl around another sharp corner at top speed. I lean to the right, digging my claws into the plastic plate with all my strength …

Did we just clip the kerb?

I'm beginning to have serious doubts about this 'professional'. It suddenly seems less likely that taking corners on the wrong side of the road counts as an advanced technique. I don't know quite how to tell you this, but I am moments away from losing my grip. The person in charge of this car is a maniac.

Now don't panic, but the tyres are screeching and there's smoke that smells of burning rubber and *I've just been flipped into a handstand against the number plate.* I can't … hold on and I'm —

— *tumbling through the aaaiiiir!*

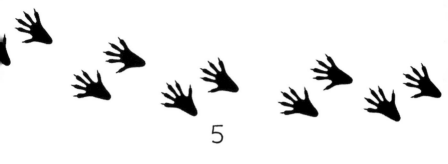

5

The Mole

My head hurts. I can't tell how long I've been lying here by the kerb, but the sun seems to have dimmed a little. I wriggle my toes to get the feeling back into them.

Normally I'd spring straight up on to the pavement, but at the moment I'll just have to climb. Which, actually, is a very smart thing to do, since it allows me time to scan this way and that for any sign of trouble. There is none. I was wise to lay low for a while – even if I did happen to be knocked out at the time.

At the far side of the pavement there are railings: tall, black, wrought-iron railings, with lots of bushes on the other side. Just a short distance away, the railings become gates. The gates are open. So I steal along the pavement and peer through the wide gateway.

It is a park. A vast green space, dotted with trees. I'm sure there will be someone in here who can point me in the direction of the Big City. I will ask anyone who is not a squirrel.

As I make my way across the park, I must confess that I am feeling rather small. You must remember that I have spent my whole life until now inside a cage, or rolling from one room to the next in a tiny plastic ball. Now I find myself thinking how huge and strange the world is.

Of course, I have plenty of time to think, because being a hamster I have fairly short legs, and so my journey across this park is not a quick one. But not to worry – I can make out something of interest, right up ahead.

What we have here is a cluster of mounds of earth, dotted around a large patch of the grass. The heap nearest to me keeps erupting like a tiny volcano, spurting clumps of dirt. I step back to avoid being showered in soil. As I do so, a huge paw like a spade with toenails sticks out from the top of the mound. It is just as I thought: these are molehills, and the critter with the foot is none other than the mole.

And there's his face. I cannot make out the eyes in his black velvet head, but he seems to be looking somewhere off to his left.

'Hello there!' I shout.

The mole freezes. Then his whiskers twitch

nervously, and his big, dirt-speckled nose sniffs the air. 'Er, hello where?'

'Down here, of course! Right in front of you!'

Finally, he is looking right in front of him. He's a bit odd, this fellow.

'What are you?' he asks. Perhaps this is a game he likes to play.

'A Syrian hamster, white and gold and fluffy, and free at last!' I say, and chuckle. 'And what are *you*?'

'I'm just a mole! A simple mole!' He claps one of those massive hands over his mouth and seems to be trying very hard not to say something more.

'A simple mole. Exactly.' Time to change the subject, I think. 'Actually, I was wondering if you might be able to help me. I'm looking for some huge gangs of murderous rats.'

His face – even without the eyes, which must be there somewhere – is a picture of total fear.

'So – can you help me?'

'Yes! I can!' He is trembling. 'You have to leave!'

He disappears back into the mound. It is very peculiar; he admits he can help me, yet refuses to do so. I must learn all that he knows. So it's into the mole hole, and away we go.

As you probably know, we hamsters are excellent diggers, so following my new friend into his underground home is no trouble at all. In fact, the mole has done a wonderful job of creating smooth, spacious tunnels. It's really quite a maze. Thankfully, little shafts of daylight are cutting through the molehills above, so I can just about see where I'm going.

I reach a junction between six different tunnels. I have no idea which way the mole went, so I pick a tunnel and head off down it.

Another junction. I'll take a right.

Now a crossroads. I'll go … left. No – straight ahead. The path there looks better trodden.

Now right again. Now left.

I am lost.

So I stop and listen. And then I listen harder.

Is that the sound of someone panting? Yes, it is. It's coming from behind me.

As I turn around, my face collides with the mole's big snout. He lets out a gasp.

'I'm Rocco,' I tell him. 'I'm sorry to barge in like this, but you did say you can help me.'

'I did.' He sounds completely defeated.

'What's your name?'

'It's …' Either he can't remember his name, or he's trying very hard not to tell it to me. 'Dwayne!'

'Hi Dwayne.'

'Look – I haven't seen any gangs or rats or gangs of rats!'

'But you know where they live?'

'YES!'

'Well that's great.'

Silence.

'So where do they live?'

'There are gangs of them everywhere in the city.'

'Okay.' I think for a moment. 'So where's the *biggest* gang?'

'The biggest? The most feared …?'

'Uh-huh.'

He sighs. 'Well that's the Big Cheese's gang.'

The Big Cheese. Such a mysterious name: it speaks of fame, and power, and … cheese. Dwayne has stopped again.

'And where do *they* live?'

'Down by the docks!' He clenches his trembling fists. 'AARRGH!'

Another silence.

'Are you all right?'

'Please! You must promise not to tell them I talked to you.'

'Of course. I promise.' Exactly what the panic is, I can't be sure. 'Really, there's nothing to worry about,' I tell him. 'Once I join the gang and I'm chosen as leader, we will live in harmony with all peaceful folk.'

It's hard to make out Dwayne's expression in the near-dark, but I can tell that it is one of surprise and, doubtless, admiration.

'Just … don't tell them.'

Dwayne seems more than happy to lead the way out of the maze, and I congratulate him on his excellent tunnels. He was, after all, very helpful, if a little hard work. In any case, I know now exactly where it is that I need to go.

I look forward to my first glimpse of the docks.

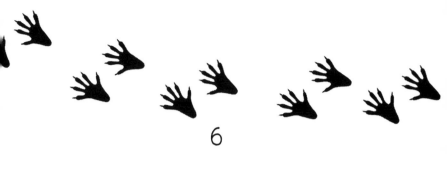

6

Drained

I must have left the park on the opposite side from where I entered, because this is definitely not the same street. It is a broad, straight road – and despite the spell of warm summer weather we've been having, it is streaming with water. To my left, I can see the reason why. A burst water main is sending a frothy plume high into the air. With the sun behind it, the water is like a sparkling golden fountain.

Looking downstream, I can make out a distant line of trees marking the end of this street, and beyond those trees, tall buildings. I'll bet *that*, right there, is the way to the docks. Of course, I've no way of knowing how far there is still to go – so I'm already on the lookout for my next transport solution.

The torrent of water is rushing in the same direction that I need to go. I watch it bubbling around the drains. As I hurry along the kerb, I can hear it gurgling and gushing below. I stop by the next drain. I watch various bits and pieces – leaves, small twigs, a chocolate wrapper – sail by on the current before dropping through the metal grating.

It might be highly dangerous down there, but you don't get to be fantastic by worrying about such details. So I hold my nose, and jump.

And then I let go of my nose, because although, in theory, I just dived easily through the grating, in actual fact I am wedged between two metal bars, staring into a watery nothingness while my rear end is warmed by the evening sun.

Fear not. With some determined wriggling, I can already feel myself slipping through. Now all I have to do is breathe in …

It's work—!

No need— for alarm— Water's very— fast. Keep getting— pushed under— Deep breath and— back in a minute—

… Just a second … till I get my breath back …

All of that may have sounded like a hamster in peril, but there was nothing to worry about. You see, Gary's mum once gave me a bath after Gary tried to turn me into a radioactive superhamster with the help of some bright green paint. So I do have experience when it comes to underwater survival.

And now I have a crushed cola can to hold on to, which is pulling me along at a fair speed. Now, if there's one valuable thing that my time with Gary has given me (other than the ability not to drown), it's the knowledge gained from that great window on the world: the television. And of the many things I saw while watching Gary's television, the sport of *surfing* is now on my mind.

All I have to do is climb on top of the flattened can, and take control …

Which is harder than it sounds, actually. As I try to scramble on, the can keeps tipping up and flipping over, so that I end up underneath it and back under the water. Finally, I haul myself on top. Then, very slowly … I stand up. Yes, I stand on my two back feet, just like a top human surfer. Well, not exactly like a top human surfer, because I'm not so much poised on my paws as resting on my rump. But if I hold my arms out, like so, the effect is pretty much the same.

You get the idea. The point is, the water is still moving fast, but I'm balancing. And now I can see light up ahead.

I seem to be gaining more and more speed as I whizz towards the end of the pipe. So this is it: the moment of truth. I would hold on tight if there was anything to hold on to, but as there isn't, I'll make do with closing my eyes … I can feel the fresh –

Aaaaah!

Oomph.

I'm lying face down, in a stream of water that is less than pure.

I sit up painfully. The water from my drainpipe is pouring into what looks to me like the sea. Which is good, because I do know that *dock* equals *water*. I also know that the giant buildings looming over me are a sure sign that I've arrived, at last, in the grimy city, just as the sun is going down.

I am wet, and I am grubby. But I've come a long way to get here, and I'm ready to begin.

7

Nev

It is completely dark. I'm sniffing my way around an alley – the thirty-third that I've explored tonight. I've been searching non-stop for any signs of life (although I did take a quick bath in a doggy water bowl outside a pub, because first impressions will be very important when I meet the gang). I am admirably clean, impressively fluffy, and totally bored.

Worst of all, suddenly it seems like the first grey glimmer of dawn is reflecting off the bins. As I pick a path between the potholes in yet another broken backstreet, I'm beginning to wonder if I might as well go to sleep and wait for daylight. After all, we hamsters always take care to get plenty of sleep. Maybe I'll just curl up for a bit, right over —

Wait. What was that? There it is again. It is a little beam of light, flickering close to the ground among the rubbish from two overflowing bins.

As I creep closer I can make out a small figure beneath the beam, scurrying to and fro. Is it a mouse? Yes, it is: a rather skinny grey mouse. The light is coming from what looks like a tiny torch, tied to his back with a piece of string.

'Excuse me!' I shout.

The light goes out. The mouse has disappeared, but I know he's there somewhere. I'll try a different approach.

'Hello? I don't mean to interrupt, but I was hoping you might be able to help me. I'm lost, you see.'

The light is back. It is shining from under an upturned cardboard box. I can see the mouse's face peering out, but he now looks more puzzled than wary.

'I'm sorry,' he says, 'but … aren't you a hamster?'

'I sure am. My name's Rocco.'

'Oh. I'm Nev.'

'What are you doing there, Nev? With the light, I mean.'

'I'm foraging.'

'Foraging?'

I don't know what that means. It's not a good feeling.

'Yeah.' He comes out from under the box and looks at me closely. 'Oh, I'm sorry. I forgot you're a pet. Foraging means looking for food.'

'Actually, I am *not* a pet. Not any more!' I puff out my chest. 'Just yesterday, I escaped from the worst small human you could ever imagine and journeyed here, all the way from the suburbs. So I would very much like to join you in a spot of foraging.'

'Okay,' says Nev, although he looks a bit unconvinced. He starts rooting around in the rubbish and is soon nibbling on something.

Of course, since leaving Gary's house I have been snacking, but my cheek pouches are still fairly stuffed with hamster food. The time has come to ditch these leftovers from my past life and stock up with the proper nosh of a wild rodent. So I'm picking my muesli and choc drops out of my cheeks and piling them on one side.

Nev stares at my little heap. 'What's all that?' he asks.

'Remnants of my dark days,' I reply, 'taken from the bowl in my cage for my epic journey. But I won't be needing them any more.'

'Are you kidding?' Nev holds out what looks like a mouldy cracker. 'We're eating rubbish out of bins. What you've got there is *food*.'

He does seem rather hungry.

'Of course,' I say quickly. 'What I mean is, I won't be needing to stow them in my cheek pouches any longer, now that I've found a friend to share them with. Please, help yourself.'

'Thank you.' Nev picks up a choc drop and takes a bite. 'Mmmm,' he says. 'Did you say that you're lost?'

'I did. I'm looking for some rats.'

'Rats?'

'A gang of rats. The Big Cheese's gang, to be precise. Do you know them?'

Nev hesitates. In fact, if it were possible, I'd swear that beneath his grey fur he's turned a little pale.

'You could say that. I'm one of the Big Cheese's mice.'

'You mean you're a gang member?'

'Sort of. Well, really the rats just tolerate our existence.' He thinks. 'No. It's not even that. We help them find food, raid restaurant kitchens. I mean, they do that too, of course – they have big appetites. But we can bring them extra, we can fit through small gaps, get into cupboards and other places that they just can't. And we stay loyal to the gang. In exchange ... well, in exchange they tolerate our existence.'

'But you *are* a gangster?'

'Not really, no.'

I think about all this for a moment. 'So you're finding food for them right now?'

'No. I took them food two days ago and it upset their stomachs, so now I'm laying low for a bit. To be honest, I can't understand how it made them ill. It was such a nice piece of beef Wellington, from one of their favourite restaurants.'

Beef Wellington. I saw that once on a cookery show that Gary's mum was watching.

'You mean the rats eat human food? As in cooked things?'

Nev stares at me in surprise. 'Of course,' he says. 'The Big Cheese is very choosy when it comes to fine dining. None of them would eat stuff like this.' He looks sadly at the mouldy cracker lying on the ground. 'Or even this,' he adds, nodding towards the last morsel of choc drop in his hand. 'No offence.'

'None taken. So,' I ask him, 'how much longer do you think you need to stay away?'

'Oh, I'm going back today. The rats don't remember anything for long.'

'Well even if they did ...' I puff out my chest again. 'This time you'll have *me* for backup.'

'Look,' says Nev, 'you really don't want to meet these rats. Trust me.'

'Ah, but I *do* want to meet them.'

'Why?'

'Because I'm going to join the gang.'

Nev laughs. But perhaps my expression shows just how serious I am, because his smile quickly fades.

'You're serious.'

'Of course I'm serious.'

'If you ask to join, they'll chop you into little pieces, just for fun.'

'Ah, but if you only knew what challenges I've overcome just to get here, you wouldn't underestimate me.'

Nev looks doubtful – but I can tell that he wants to be convinced.

'Well you can't stick around here, that's for sure.' He thinks for a moment. 'Okay. I'll take you back to the docklands with me. On the way, you can tell me all about these adventures of yours. Then I'll think about it. Whether to take you to the gang, I mean.'

And so at last, I'm on my way. As we head out of the alley and back on to the street, a pink sunrise is spreading through the sky. It's going to be a good day.

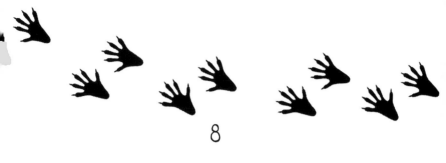

8

Restaurants, Rats and a Rumpus

We are riding in the back of a van, surrounded by bottles of milk. I've just finished telling Nev all about everything – from how I defeated both cat and dog in single combat to my daredevil surfing in the sewer. I'm surprised to hear that he has met Dwayne several times, though he won't say much about how it is they know each other.

'So,' I ask at last, 'will you take me to see the rats?'

Nev shrugs. How could he say no?

The van comes to a stop. The driver's door opens, and bangs shut. Footsteps. I hold my breath as daylight floods the inside of the van. Nev springs lightly through the open doors and scurries away along the pavement.

My turn.

I jump. Land with a bit of a forward roll. Pick myself up and hurry after the mouse. He's waiting for me on the corner of the street.

'Well here we are,' says Nev. 'Welcome to the docklands.'

I look around. The docklands are a big surprise, and a bit of a disappointment. Far from being the drab slimy hole I had imagined, the gang's territory is stuffed with fancy restaurants. Many of these have brightly coloured awnings over their windows and doors, or outdoor tables under large umbrellas. They line the streets on either side of a river crossed by a bridge. The river, mind you, is dark, dirty and sluggish, so at least that's something.

As we make our way towards the bridge, I am happy to see that our destination lies somewhere in the shadowy damp beneath it. We run freely across the banking at the water's edge; although it is a bright and sunny morning, this early on a Sunday there is scarcely anyone around. Even so, Nev seems tense.

He stops beside a hole in the concrete, just under the bridge. The end of a pipe sticks out of it. A thin line of water trickles from the pipe and dribbles down the banking. Nev hesitates.

'Now remember,' he says, 'whatever you do, don't tell them that you're here to become some sort of gangster. Say that you want to be like us mice – help them out in exchange for a roof over your head.'

'Can I tell them that I want to be the greatest hamster that ever lived, and inspire other rodents to take up the quest for greatness?'

'No.' This is a historic moment; I wish Nev would stop looking so worried about it. 'Are you sure you want to go in there?'

'Yes.'

'Only if you're sure.'

'Absolutely I'm sure.'

'Well … okay then.'

He enters the pipe. I follow.

There is a curious stale smell and a sound of loud, arguing voices. As we move further along, I can see a faint light up ahead. It is coming from an opening on the right.

Just short of the opening, Nev raises a hand, signalling me to stop. He peers inside. 'Wait here,' he whispers.

He disappears through the opening. I press my ear to the wall of the pipe. I can hear Nev clear his throat.

'Everyone!' he shouts. 'Listen up a minute!'

From the noise levels in there, I'd say nobody is listening up.

'I'VE BROUGHT A NEWBIE!'

Silence. I can hear my own heart pounding.

'He's … not a rat. Or a mouse. But he wants to be a mouse. I mean —'

There are rumblings of angry voices. I fear that

Nev may be losing his cool.

'He doesn't want to be a rat! I mean a gangster!'

It's only right that I should help him out. So I bowl through the opening, ready to work the crowd.

'Greetings!' I shout. 'I am Rocco, and I am here to find you food, just as though I were a mouse, in exchange for your roof over my head and your tolerance of my existence!'

I pause for dramatic emphasis. We have entered a vast candlelit chamber, full of enormous rats in various shades of black, brown and grey. Up the back, a group of mice are staring open-mouthed. I assume these are Nev's family, so I give them a friendly wave. One of them waves back.

'What's *this* then?' Finally, someone is returning my greeting. 'Suburban FLUFF wants us to *tolerate his existence*. Sounds awfully like he expects us not to send him to the bottom of the deep blue dock, does it not?'

The speaker is a large and scrawny rat with a long, bent nose, crooked teeth and cross eyes. Each of those eyes is bloodshot. Quite simply, he's the strangest fellow I've ever seen.

'Actually, I'm a Syrian hamster,' I tell him. The rats begin to laugh.

'It wouldn't make sense to drown him, Minestroni!' cries Nev. Minestroni must be the scrawny rat. I have to admit, I missed the bit when he said anything about drowning me. 'He *is* from the suburbs,' Nev continues, 'but that's just it! This hamster thwarted man, defeated dog and overcame cat just to get here!'

All at once, the rats begin murmuring among themselves. I give Nev a thumbs up, because what he just said showed some serious style.

'Enough, enough, enough!' Minestroni claps his hands for silence. 'This *character*' – he is pointing a long, hooked claw in my direction – 'has a *nerve* that is about to get him what he wants *or* get him exceptionally dead. But we all know whose decision that will be.' Now it's his turn to pause for effect, but the rats only grumble impatiently. Minestroni jabs his finger at me. 'Stay there,' he says importantly, 'while I speak with the Big Cheese.'

He disappears through a wide crack in the wall. The other rats turn and eye Nev and me with toothy grins. Of course, everyone told me this would happen – this business of the rats wanting to kill me – but somehow I figured that when the moment arrived I would spontaneously work out what to do in order to survive.

It occurs to me that this is that moment. And that my mind is curiously blank.

'Listen,' says Nev, 'if this all goes badly, *run*.'

'Are we about to see the Big Cheese?' I ask.

Nev looks at me in astonishment. 'Nobody ever sees the Big Cheese. Except Minestroni, of course. He's the Big Cheese's right-hand rat. No one else is allowed in his presence.'

'Why not?'

'For security reasons.'

This is fascinating: the Big Cheese must be even more amazingly important than I thought.

'OI, OI, OI!'

Once again everyone in the chamber goes quiet. The harsh, booming voice seems to be coming from a hole halfway up the wall. As I look more closely I can see that the hole is in fact the end of a metal pipe, like a big mouth, round and black and perfectly shaped for shouting.

I look at Nev, who knows exactly what I'm thinking.

'Yes,' he says, 'that's him.'

''OO DO WE 'AVE 'ERE THEN, EH? WOSS ALL THIS ABOUT AN '*AMSTER* THAT WANTS TO BE TOLERANT?'

There is a faint whispering at the other end of the pipe.

'TOLERATED!'

The voice echoes around the walls. A few flecks of stone and dirt flutter from above. I take a deep breath.

'I am Rocco, sir! Rocco the Fantastic! I wish to join with your mice! I offer my legendary foraging skills, and my built-in high-capacity haute cuisine receptacles!'

I stuff my hands inside my cheeks and push them out to reveal their impressive food-carrying capacity. Then I remember that the Big Cheese can't actually see me, so I turn this way and that to show the other rats and get them to back me up. Surprisingly, they do no such thing (raised eyebrows and scowling aren't much help), but now there's a *lot* of whispering going on in that pipe.

'AND WHY,' asks the voice at last, 'WOULD WE BE NEEDIN' YOU TO GO ALL THE WAY OUT THERE LOOKIN' FOR GRUB, WHEN I'LL BET YOU'RE AS PLUMP AND JUICY A MORSEL AS ANY THAT EVER CAME OUT OF CHEF CLAUDE'S KITCHEN!'

I have no idea who Chef Claude is, but this time the death threat is loud and clear. From the corner of my eye I can see Nev mouthing something. I think it's got to do with the plan he suggested a minute ago. But I've an idea of my own.

'Now listen here!' I shout boldly. 'You mistake me for a snack, but I'll stick in your throat and play your molars like a xylophone, if I have to! I'll find a thousand ways to cook Chef Claude before breakfast! I AM THE HAMSTER GANGSTER!'

The rats stare in disbelief. Nev is shaking, with a look on his face that suggests he is being throttled by a pair of invisible hands.

'Give me a week,' I tell them, 'and every animal in this town will know my name. *My* fierce reputation will be *your* fierce reputation!'

I'm really quite pleased with how that came out.

'ARE YOU SERIOUS?!!' The Big Cheese's yell screams in the pipe. A few in the crowd cover their ears. 'DO YOU REALLY THINK *THIS GANG* NEEDS 'ELP FROM SOME *POCKET-MONEY PET* TO BE FAMOUS?!!'

'No, I don't. But you do not want me to take my awesome brilliance elsewhere. I hear there are plenty other gangs around here who would be grateful for it.'

An angry murmur spreads through the crowd. Several dozen pairs of eyes gleam dangerously in the candlelight.

'IS THAT SO. WELL YOU LISTEN 'ERE, AND LISTEN GOOD. YOU WANNA BRING US FOOD? YOU CAN JOLLY WELL GET US FOOD. STARTIN' WITH THE NICE LITTLE BIT OF CHEESE IN THE MOUSETRAP IN CHEF CLAUDE'S KITCHEN.'

The other rats are giggling. I've no idea what a 'mousetrap' is, but clearly I'm to assume that this will not be an easy task.

'And if I succeed?'

'IF YOU SUCCEED!' The Big Cheese roars with laughter, and all but the mice do the same.

'IF YOU SUCCEED THEN YOU CAN BRING US ALL THE GRUB YOU LIKE. YOU CAN CHEW UP EVERY OTHER GANG IN TOWN AND BRING 'EM 'ERE STASHED IN THAT FAT LITTLE FACE OF YOURS, IF THAT'S WHAT YOU'RE MADE OF.'

'You mean I'll be in the gang?'

'I *MEAN* YOU'LL BE IN THE *GANG*.'

For a moment there I was ready to shout, 'Thank you very much!' but I suppose that's not the kind of thing a hard-as-nails gangster should say.

'You've got a deal!'

Much better.

Anyway, no one is listening. Already the rats are shouting or joking or arguing among themselves, while the mice are shuffling from the room, shaking their heads. All except two, that is. Nev is still standing next to me with a worried look on his face, and just behind him, a small mouse stares at me in fascination. She has a piece of pink shoelace tied around her head like a bandana.

'So,' I ask them, 'can someone please show me the way to Chef Claude's kitchen?'

Nev raises his hand, then faints.

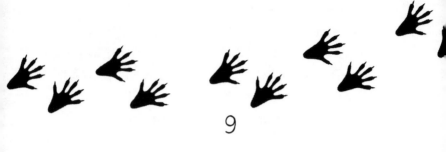

9

The Mousetrap

Back out on the street, I have to say I don't think much of Chef Claude's restaurant. It has sickly bright awnings, and *Claude's* written in fancy scribbles on the windows.

'It's a bit small,' I remark.

'It's a traditional French bistro,' replies Nev. 'People come here from all across the city and beyond.'

I can tell that there are moments when he thinks me ignorant. The mouse in pink headgear, meanwhile, has turned out to be Nev's little sister, Tina. She is a couple of feet away, kicking the air and slicing it with her hands, apparently practising some kind of martial art.

'I do not doubt that the food is *très bien*,' I continue, 'but I cannot believe that a place with so many frills could be filled with danger.'

Nev glares at me. 'Look, Rocco, around these parts to be a rodent is to be a *pest*. Everybody wants you *dead*, and you obviously have no idea how good these people are at getting what they want.'

'But I'm a hamster.'

'Oh, that's right. I'm so sorry. I forgot that you're an invincible world-beating *hamster*.'

Actually, that's not what I was talking about. I simply meant that the humans might not see me as disease-ridden vermin. But Nev hasn't finished.

'In fact, since grabbing the cheese is going to be so easy for you, why *don't* you just cook Chef Claude a thousand ways while you're at it. There's still plenty of time before breakfast.'

I take one last look at the candy-striped canvas over the door and windows. 'Maybe I will.'

Nev storms off towards the rear of the restaurant. I hurry after him, closely followed by Tina. We stop by the back door, which is wedged wide open. I can hear the sound of chopping, and somebody shouting in an angry form of French. Nev sniffs the air.

'They're preparing for a busy brunch service,' he says. He hops on to the low step and peers cautiously around the door. I move to follow, but in the same instant Nev turns and rushes back out. 'I saw it!' he hisses. 'We have to get out of here!'

'You saw what?'

'The *mousetrap*! It's one of the nastiest I've ever seen, and I've seen a lot of mousetraps.'

I'm still trying to imagine what this thing must look like. Nev's opinion of it has only made me more eager to find out.

'Let me see.'

'Rocco …'

Before he can say any more, I make a dash for the door. I stop on the threshold and survey the scene. 'Is it the little piece of wood on the floor, with a lump of cheddar on top?'

For a moment Nev says nothing. Once again, I fear, he is annoyed by the disappointment in my voice.

'Let me tell you why we're here,' he says. 'We're here because back in that sewer you did such an outstanding job of almost getting us both killed that I had a strong desire to throw you into the jaws of that mousetrap myself. But I got over that. Then I thought maybe if I showed you what it is we're dealing with, you'd see sense and abandon the whole idea. Clearly, I was wrong. So you're just going to have to believe me when I say that if you go in there that *little piece of wood* is going to snap your face off.'

'I highly doubt that.'

'Well don't. Why do you think the Big Cheese sent you here?'

'Because the Big Cheese thinks that just

'cause *he's* too daft to get the cheese out that trap, everyone else must be too.'

Those last words were Tina's, although I couldn't have put it better myself.

'Tina, will you please stop encouraging him?'

'You can do it, Rocco! I know you can!'

'Thank you. Would you like to come too?'

'NO!!'

While Nev holds back an enthusiastic Tina, I seize my chance.

'I'll be back in just a minute.'

With that, I'm straight through the door and into Chef Claude's kitchen. I find myself standing in the middle of a large orange square. It's a tiled floor – very cold underfoot. But I ignore this, just as I am ignoring the angry whispers coming from the direction of Nev.

I am still hidden from the cooks' view by the open door, but their voices are very close by. From the sound of it, there are three. One is mad with anger, while the other two keep saying, '*Oui, Chef!*' as if pleading for their lives.

I am three tiles away from the mousetrap. Creeping closer, I can see the metal arm that is poised to snap home should I try to snatch the cheese. I shiver: Nev was right. I had no idea humans could be this cruel.

I am more determined than ever to get that cheese. But how?

As the shouting gets louder, I hurry under a nearby work table. From here I can take in the whole scene above me. Other than the tiles on the floor, the entire kitchen seems to be made out of stainless steel, from the work surfaces and the refrigerator to the giant pots and rows of fearsome knives. Various utensils hang from hooks at one end of my table. Perhaps one of them could be useful to me in my task.

But my mind is annoyingly – and unusually – blank.

From my present hiding place, I see Chef Claude only as a pair of large clogs, partly hidden beneath his baggy checked trousers. From the sound of it, there is some kind of problem with *les petits pois*. A pair of skinny legs comes into view, wearing grubby trainers and hauling a large white bag of something. Chef Claude strides towards the owner of these skinny legs. His huge hands grab hold of the bag and lift it from the floor.

'ZEY ARE FROZEHN?!!'

As the other chef squeaks an apology, Claude hurls the white bag to the floor. It bursts open and a thousand green balls spill across the tiles, bouncing on the hard surface. I recognise them at once: these are peas. And they must be a force for good, because Gary hated them, and loudly refused to eat them.

I grab one as it rolls past. As my fingers close

around the freezing-cold vegetable, a bolt of pain shoots up my arm, triggering the urge to drop it and, at the same time, lighting the spark of genius in my brain. With a yell of agony heard only inside my head, I leap into the air and release the pea in an impressive overarm throw, aimed at the jaws of the mousetrap.

The pea misses and hits the wall with a soft tap. No matter. With lightning speed I scoop up an armful more, and fling them one by one at the trap.

I need to perfect my aim. On the count of three: one … two …

I release a pea. It misses. I take aim and throw another. It misses. And another …

This time the pea bounces in the middle of the mousetrap – and the metal arm of evil closes with a *snap*.

The pea is squashed flat. The chunk of cheese remains.

I am about to dash towards it – but another light bulb flicks on in my brain. Quickly I scoop up a few more armfuls of peas, one hand feeding them into my mouth at a speed I never knew hands could move at.

Now I'm ready. I run towards the trap. All I need to— *Whoa, hold on one second, there are THREE chefs in this kitchen!* I forgot about the third, but seeing him out the corner of my eye, coming this way, is a helpful reminder.

I dive behind a sack of potatoes. This chef is a tall man in a tall puffy hat. Obviously, he has heard the sound of the trap. He stares at the squashed pea. He looks around at all the other peas scattered across the floor, and shrugs. With that, he hurries back to his chopping board.

I pounce on the trap, wrestle the cheese free, run for the door. No looking back.

As I take a flying leap into the morning sun, Tina rushes to greet me, pounding the air with one fist. Nev looks from the cheese, to me, and back to the cheese again.

I run straight past and keep on going. The others are right behind me.

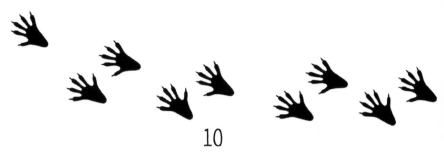

10

Cheesed Off

Let me just fill you in on what's been happening since we got back to the lair, because frankly I need to tell it to someone before I'll believe it.

After giving me the meanest look a crooked-faced sewer rat can manage, Minestroni stomped off to the Big Cheese's private quarters, taking with him my hard-won cheese. Honestly – not a single word of amazement that I'd managed to get it, or even a simple 'well done'. And now that we're awaiting the boss rat's response, all the other members of the gang are looking at me not with admiration, but with even more nastiness than before.

All we can hear are the usual angry whispers coming from the pipe. This has been going on for several minutes.

'WOSS THIS THEN?' says the Big Cheese, finally. 'THE CHEESE FROM CHEF CLAUDE'S TRAP?'

'Of course it is. That's what you asked for.'

'AND YOU COULDN'T 'AVE LAID THEM DAINTY PAWS OF YOURS ON SOMETHIN' TASTY, COULD YA? YOU COULDN'T 'AVE BROUGHT ME SOME OF THAT HAUTE CUISINE THEY GOT LITTERED ABOUT THAT KITCHEN. NO. YOU 'AD TO BRING ME THIS *RUBBISH*.'

'Yes! Because the whole *point* was to get out with *that cheese*. So that's exactly what I did.'

'That's exactly what he did.' Tina gets the words out just as Nev claps a hand over her mouth.

'But since you mention it,' I add grudgingly, 'I did bring back something else.' I spit the petits pois out quick-fire, like bullets. Thankfully they have defrosted in my cheeks, and the rats round about seem to think them rather good.

'Thirty-six freshly frozen petits pois,' I declare.

'WELL, YOU'VE GOT SOME SHOPPIN' BAGS, I'LL GIVE YOU THAT. BUT YOU'LL DO BETTER THAN RAW VEG NEXT TIME, IF YOU KNOW WHAT'S GOOD FOR YA.'

I hope that he's remembering our deal.

'Does that mean I'm in the gang? I mean, as a mouse, yes, but as a rat as well?'

'IT MEANS YOU'RE AT THE BOTTOM OF THE FOOD CHAIN, AND YOU'LL DO WHAT YOU'RE TOLD THEN MAKE YOURSELF SCARCE, IF YOU KNOW WHAT'S GOOD FOR YA.'

I'll take that as a yes – and a massive let-down. Is this really to be my triumphant moment of joining the gang? Have I beaten my fearsome housemates, ridden a four-wheeled death trap and been flushed through a sewer just to be put down by a greedy rat whose only threat is *if you know what's good for you*?

Apparently so. Everyone is drifting out of the chamber, including Nev and Tina, who are signalling me to follow. It's enough to make anyone yearn for a cage full of sweet-smelling sawdust to sink into.

But thankfully, I am not just anyone. I am Rocco, and I'll make sure these rats get to grips with that if it's the last thing I ever do.

I like Nev's family. His parents, Uncle Alfie and Cousin Pip, along with him and Tina, make up the gang's entire mouse population. We are sitting in their home, the mouse house – little more than a collection of matchbox beds beneath a manhole – munching on Edam cheese. Everyone is looking at me with a great curiosity.

'One thing I've always wanted to know about

living in a cage,' says Uncle Alfie, 'is where do you go when you need to … you know … *go*?'

'For goodness' sake, Alfie, don't ask such questions,' says Nev's mum.

'It's quite all right,' I tell them. 'You simply choose a corner of the cage, and go there. Except for sometimes – quite often actually – when it's more convenient to go elsewhere.'

Everyone looks disgusted, which is a bit worrying given that *they* live in a sewer. Perhaps it's time to change the subject.

'So,' I begin, 'is everyone ready for the future? It's going to be a bit less rat and a lot more hamster.'

Nev's dad looks interested. 'You mean, *going* where we like?'

'No. Well, yes. But I mean fewer death threats and more incredible heroics.'

'But *how*?' asks a wide-eyed Tina.

'I don't know yet. But don't worry about that. In my experience, if you go looking for adventure, things *happen*. Pretty soon I'll be famous, and ours will be the gang that everyone wants to join and no one wants to mess with.'

Tina has a faraway look in her eyes, but Nev's look is boring straight into me. Thankfully, though, we're all being distracted by Cousin Pip, who has brought a half-eaten chocolate éclair from a nearby café.

As we share out the éclair, a vague, fleeting memory of my mother and my five brothers and sisters flashes in my head. I don't know why; I suppose it's just being with the mice that made me think for a moment of my own long-lost family.

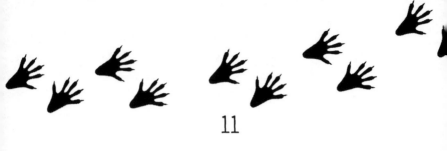

11

On Friends and Foes

Today is my first day as a gangster. Last night after we polished off the chocolate éclair, Nev filled me in on a few details about the gang's business. It's a simple but very clever one of giving protection to less indestructible animals in exchange for some kind of payment. Now get this: our single biggest client is a group of foxes … I'll let that sink in a moment … That's right – *foxes*! Of course, you're wondering why big, cunning foxes need to be protected by rodents.

Come to think of it, so am I. But I guess we'll find out soon enough, because right now my fellow rats and I are out on patrol, and we're marching right into the foxes' territory. It's a wide yard with a pair of disused sheds on one side. Naturally, we are armed with the most terrifying stolen weaponry, including spatulas and dessert spoons.

Okay, so the first thing I'm noticing is that these foxes seem to love seafood, probably collected from the fine seafood restaurants round about. There are old ice cream tubs brimming with anchovies, baskets of things in shells, a tray full of silver fish many times my size.

One of the foxes steps out of the nearest shed. I spring on to my haunches, waving my pastry brush (yes, okay, so the others grabbed all the scarier weapons). But the fox is approaching at a dainty trot, and is clearly not a threat.

'Good afternoon!' he says brightly. 'You are more than welcome. We have collected a great deal of seafood this lunchtime, and are in need of your help to put the thieves off thieving.'

Put the thieves *off*? The Hamster Gangster did not come here to put enemies *off*, but to defeat them in some serious action.

There's a lot of squawking overhead, which is really annoying me right now.

I look up.

Hmm. It seems the foxes are not the only ones who like a well-cooked mussel. At least a dozen seagulls are circling up there, determined to thieve everyone else's food rather than find their own. Clearly, the reputation of the Big Cheese's gang is enough to keep these bullies away. So we're standing perfectly still, while the foxes stash their smelly leftovers in the sheds.

There's a sudden flash of movement in the sky. Wait a second – big feathery —

'DIVE-BOMBERS!!' I yell.

Four of them!

Heading straight for us rats!

Sunlight flashes on stainless steel. Gulls are screeching, feathers flying. They flap their wings hard, trying to beat us back. I hop up and down, jabbing upwards with my pastry brush. But I can't reach high enough, because the rats are hemming me in.

One of them leaps up, armed with an ice cream scoop.

He lands right on top of me.

As I stare between the rats' legs, I count eight more seagulls, gathered around a crate of fish. As soon as the rat scrambles off me, I grab my brush between my jaws and crawl out of the fray. Now I can see them clearly: a flock of big gulls, busy plucking fish from the crate while their friends keep the rats distracted. Four foxes sit glowering in the rats' direction, clearly intent on complaining about poor service rather than doing anything about it themselves.

I sprint towards the crate, swift and silent … Now I'm right alongside one of the gulls. I take my pastry brush from between my teeth … and whack him with the handle across his big ugly beak. He wails, and spreads his wings – but I'm already off and running.

'OVER HERE!!' I shout to the rats. 'THEY'RE ATTACKING TO CREATE A DIVER—'

Okay. So one of the gulls has just dropped a large fish on me, and once again I am pinned down. It's dark, and a bit stinky under here. But I can hear a muffled commotion all around.

There is nothing to do but wait.

And wait.

The commotion has stopped.

Still waiting.

The fish is lifted off me. I jump to my feet – but there is no sign of the gulls. The rats stand about with satisfied faces. I turn to the fox who lifted away the fish, the same one who greeted us. Naturally, because I rescued the situation, it would be wrong for me to thank him. So instead I'll simply finish what I was saying:

'A *diversion*.'

'Quite right,' says the fox. He holds out his paw towards me. 'My name is Maurice.'

I shake his claw. 'Rocco,' I tell him.

I turn to the rats for some praise and congratulations, but most of them are already starting to leave. In fact, the only ones paying me any attention are Minestroni and a lanky rat behind him. Both are glaring at me with all the menace they can muster.

Clearly, in this gang being brilliant is not the same thing as being popular.

I've told Nev everything that happened today, although I left out the detail about Minestroni and the lanky rat, because he does get so nervous. When I first bowled into the mouse house, Nev was the only one home, and he greeted me with wide eyes, saying, 'Rocco! You're alive!' in a very surprised tone of voice. But he has listened to my story with a kind of cautious approval, and says that my becoming trapped under a dead fish was very fortunate. I disagree with this, but I won't argue, because I'm desperate to learn more from him.

For starters, the foxes remain a bit of a mystery.

'They've no interest in fighting,' Nev explains.

'And no talent for it either, I daresay.'

'No.'

'And how do they pay us?' I ask. 'What do we get in return for helping them?'

'Well …' Nev sighs. It seems like he's about to tell me something he's been trying hard *not* to tell me. 'Don't get excited, Rocco …' Now I'm *really* excited. 'There's a gang of alley cats. Big, mean critters, all scarred faces and chewed-off ears. They're desperate to come in, wipe out the rats and take over the docklands. Yet they don't even try.'

'Why not?' I breathe. 'If they're so tough, why don't they try?'

'Because the foxes pretend to be the rats' sly and vicious allies. When they're out and about, the foxes are not the twinkle-toed characters you saw today. They slink through the streets with toothy grins on their faces. That's the price they have to pay for the rats' protection.'

'Wow.'

'Indeed.'

'And are there any other enemies to look out for?'

Nev thinks for a moment. 'Well, there's a shady pigeon named Francis Pigeoni. He spies on each gang's every move and reports it to their rivals. The thing is, he does this to *everyone*; he's spying on one gang even as he's telling them the latest news about their enemies. Every gang would want to kill him for his double-crossing, if he wasn't so ... well, useful.'

'But he's never found out what the foxes are really like? Otherwise he'd have told all of that to the alley cats.'

'Exactly. The foxes keep a very careful lookout for him. Of course, he'd soon find out the truth if the seagulls had the brains to share it with him. We're lucky they're the dimmest wits in the docks.'

Lucky indeed. All this incredible information

is swirling in my brain – but there's still room in there for a brilliant idea.

'Why don't we have our very *own* spy?' I ask. 'Someone who works for our gang, and our gang only?'

'Ah, well. You remember Dwayne?' Nev asks.

'Of course.'

'He works for us. We rely on Dwayne for nearly all our intelligence.'

'Is that a good idea? He didn't seem very switched on when I met him.'

'No,' says Nev, 'not that kind of intelligence. I mean we need him to *gather* intelligence. Find out everything we need to know about the other gangs, all over town. *Dwayne's* our spy. His network of tunnels doesn't just criss-cross the park, it reaches across most of the city. He spies only for the rats. If he were to talk to anyone else, the rats would be after him. That's why he's so nervous about speaking to strangers, you see. Dwayne is unable to tell a lie. He absolutely cannot stop himself from spilling the whole truth.'

'Oh. That certainly explains a lot.' Then I remember something. 'Ah, but he *can* tell a lie. He told me that he's never seen any gangs of rats. That can't be true, not if he's working for us.'

'Actually, it can,' says Nev. 'Dwayne is completely blind.'

'A blind spy?'

'Yep. He sniffs the enemy out, then listens in on what they're saying.'

I'm so glad to hear that Dwayne is one of us, and I hope this means we'll meet again soon. I'm sure he'll be very happy to know that I have joined the gang. Speaking of which …

'I've been noticing,' I say, 'that the rats are pretty hard to impress.'

'That's because *everyone* wants to be the next Big Cheese,' replies Nev, 'and they don't like rivals, popping up out of nowhere and threatening their chances. There are squabbles every day over where everyone fits in the pecking order. Around here, you don't rise through the ranks by winning friends, but by winning fights.'

Suddenly I'm very glad I left out that certain detail from my report of the day's events. If I were to tell Nev that I somehow upset the Big Cheese's right-hand rat on my very first day, he'd stuff me in a padded envelope and mail me straight back to the suburbs. Besides, there's no need for him to know; I have all of this under control. I will use my brainpower to prove my worth and outsmart any would-be rivals. And as you know, should anyone try any mischief I will defend myself most ably.

12

Fast Food

Breakfast.

French crêpes, filled with chocolate spread and sliced banana, served with a side order of flying knives. Note that Chef Claude can wield two rolling pins at once and still stab, throw skewers and toss pans of boiling water at small rodents. Tina is in attack mode with her martial arts, leaping and punching, very, *very* close to the medley of missiles. It's impressive, though the other mice yell at her to stop.

Also note that sitting on a chopping board while helping oneself to food on nearby plates may cause unnecessary alarm. Cousin Pip almost faints before I remind him that I only had a stump of a tail to begin with.

Lunch.

Italiano. A bottle of olive oil soaring past my ear to smash against the wall. Two lessons to learn here: one, Nev is quite right that dough balls and pepperoni are easier to carry back to the sewer than ravioli soaked in tomato sauce; and two, there are many ways to shout death threats at small animals in Italian. Weirdly, Tina has replies to them all.

Dinner.

Chinese. One cook realises I'm a (former) fluffy pet. Tries to trap me under a colander. Gets badly bitten.

Very nearly strangle myself with a noodle, but between us we get out with four dumplings, three spring rolls and a couple of cheek pouches' worth of special fried rice.

Three square meals, and a load of very satisfied rats – Big Cheese included. All in a day's work for Mouse and Hamster Catering Incorporated.

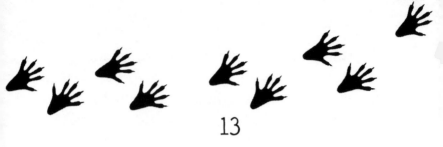

13

Pistachio Peril

Well I knew it wouldn't be long before I saw some of the squabbles that Nev described begin to play out. Now here we are, two days later, being swept along in a tide of rats hurrying towards the main chamber, all because Minestroni is apparently dead. It seems that he has choked to death on something beginning with the letter *p*.

'It's a type of nut,' Nev is trying to explain, despite the rabble of raised voices. 'And now there will be *chaos*.'

Be that as it may, Minestroni didn't seem to like me very much, and it's a bit of a relief that he's gone. I feel slightly bad about that, but not really. As we pour into the chamber, several rats are jostling for position atop the slimy brick that

Minestroni once stood on to speak to the crowd. It's turning into a riot in here.

'SHUT AAAAP!!' The Big Cheese's pipe rattles dangerously. He has everyone's attention. 'SHOW SOME RESPECT, YOU 'ARTLESS VERMIN! ME TRUSTED ADVISOR, MINESTRONI—' The Big Cheese's voice breaks up, and something like a sniffle echoes in the pipe. Everyone exchanges surprised glances. The Big Cheese clears his throat. '—MINESTRONI, HAS *PASSED AWAY*. NOW I DON'T KNOW WHICH OF YOU STOOGES DID THIS – IF I DID, I'D 'AVE YOUR GUTS ON CLAUDE'S FRENCH TOAST – BUT 'OOEVER YOU ARE, YOU 'AVE CREATED A *VACANCY*. NOW I NEEDS A NOO ADVISOR IMMEDIATELY. SO. ANYONE 'OO WANTS TO BE CONSIDERED FOR THIS POST BETTER DO SOMETHIN' SMART, AND DO IT QUICK. I DON'T CARE IF YOU DICE UP THE ALLEY CATS OR FIND ME A NICE CHOUX BUN. NOW. DOES ANYONE 'AVE ANY QUESTIONS?'

'*I* do!' Enter the rat who has managed to claim Minestroni's old brick. I recognise him as the lanky fellow who was standing right behind Minestroni after the seagulls-and-dead-fish incident. 'I say we finds out who did this to poor old Minestroni. Give him a taste of his own medicine.' An uncertain murmur drifts through the crowd. 'So who's got a guilty face, then?'

The murmuring dies away. Everyone stares awkwardly at their feet.

'Standin' up for justice are you, Vinny?' shouts a loud voice from the back of the chamber. 'Or just makin' sure that whoever did it won't be challengin' you for that there brick?'

The crowd likes this.

'Yeah!' someone else pipes up. 'How come you're up there anyway, Vinny? Bit keen on bein' the new Minestroni, are ya?'

'How long's *that* been goin' on?'

As the angry jeering gets louder, Vinny arches his back and bares his yellow teeth. I think it's time someone pointed out the silliness of all this, before anyone gets hurt.

'Actually,' I shout, 'isn't it more likely that this was just an accident?'

A hush falls over the crowd. Nev has just kicked me, which I'll take as a sign of encouragement.

'What d'you mean?' someone asks.

'What I *mean* is that you hardly need anybody's help to choke to death. I think you'll find the thing simply stuck in Minestroni's throat and killed him.'

Most of the rats seem to be thinking hard about this new concept of accidental death. You know, I think I might have prevented a disaster here.

'Seems to know an awful lot about choking, doesn't he?'

Or perhaps not. Everyone is muttering suspiciously.

'Ah yes,' sneers Vinny, 'if it ain't the cocky fluffball who so *cleverly* got the cheese out of the trap and so *daringly* fought off the seagulls from underneath a fish ...'

'HANG ON A MINUTE.' The Big Cheese sounds confused. 'ARE WE SAYIN' IT WAS THE 'AMSTER DID IT?'

'No, of course I didn't!'

'THEN WHO DID?'

'No one! That's my point!'

'YOU BETTER START MAKIN' SOME SENSE.'

'It can't have been Rocco! He was with us mice the whole time!'

Those are some very sensible words from Tina. Now the rats are accusing anyone standing near them whom they haven't seen in the past couple of hours.

'Come on,' says Nev, 'let's make ourselves scarce until things cool off.'

We slip quietly from the chamber.

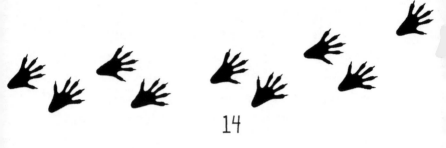

14

Dirty Tricks and Cocktail Sticks

A day has passed since Minestroni's death, and the air around here is thick with menace. Each and every rat wants to be Minestroni's replacement – and attacking anyone who might threaten one's chances seems to be the favourite strategy. Of course, yesterday's mysterious killer – surely everyone's biggest rival – continues to terrify the whole gang, despite not really existing.

Nev's family have insisted that I stay with them in the mouse house. Naturally, I am spending my time here wisely, planning my own bid for the top job. My preferred option is to single-handedly defeat the alley cats. But first I must discover their whereabouts.

Of course Nev knows exactly where they live, but there is no way he will reveal that information while he continues to doubt my capabilities. Indeed, I have been careful not to give away any hint of my plan, trying hard to keep all expressions of deep thinking off my face.

Tina might know. Where the cats live, I mean. And she won't be afraid to tell me. Happily, everyone except Tina and me is away looking for food; at this dangerous time, Tina has been told to stay behind because she is the youngest, and I because I am a target for would-be attackers. Not that those worry me, but I can't be wasting time fighting them off when I need to *think*.

Thinking time is over.

'Tina, where do the alley cats live?'

Tina stops practising her two-footed rear-end power kicks. 'One-point-two miles west, between the Scuttled Frigate pub and the twenty-four-hour minimart. In the alley!' Her eyes are wide. 'You *are* going there, aren't you?'

'Yes, actually, I am.'

'To knock them all out?'

'Pretty much.'

'I'm coming with you!'

I should have known she'd say that.

'You are a heroic spirit, Tina,' I tell her, 'and your moment to shine will come. But today I must go alone. What would Nev do, if he came back here to find us both gone?'

'He'd freak.'

'That's correct. So you have to do a very important job, and tell everyone that I've just popped out to use the bathroom. That should buy me enough time to get well on my way.'

'Okay.' Tina bites her lip, which is trembling with excitement. 'I can do that.' She runs into a shadowy corner where the mice store useful items collected on their foraging trips, and returns carrying a cocktail stick. 'Here,' she says. 'Take this for weaponry. The rats will be outside.'

I am about to say, 'No thanks, I will fight them with my bare hands,' when an image of me and my cocktail stick, caught up in some serious ninja action against four rats at once, flashes through my mind. From the gleam in her eye, I can see that Tina is thinking exactly the same thing.

'And also,' she says, 'you should take the number 32 bus. Jump off at the Scuttled Frigate.'

'Thank you, Tina. I should be back by nightfall, I expect.'

I hurry through the pipe that leads to the great outdoors with Tina's loud whispers of '*Good luck, Rocco!*' echoing behind me. After so much time in the sewer, the sunlight hurts my eyes as I come out on to the banking.

I glance this way and that. It is the middle of the day, and a steady flow of traffic is rumbling over the bridge nearby. Across the street, holidaymakers and people on their lunch breaks are seated at tables outside Perfecto's Pizzeria. To try and board the bus over there would be far too risky. Instead, I will hurry up the banking … it's a little awkward with my cocktail stick, but here we are … and I will follow the cobbled lane along the side of the Jolly Yachtsman Hotel. In three minutes and twenty seconds – make that seventeen – I will join the bus route on the much quieter street outside the old warehouse.

There's just one thing that's bothering me a little. If I didn't know any better – that is, if I didn't have a calm and rational mind – I'd swear that there are footsteps behind me. Of course, I *do* have such a mind, so I know those are not footsteps, but figments of my imagination only. They are *not* quick little footsteps, tap-tap-tapping on the cobbles. Like four sets of claws – no, eight sets of claws, divided between two sets of four feet. Four big feet on each of two big rodents. Rat-sized rodents.

When you think about it, at a time like this, taking a look over my shoulder would not be a sign of silliness. It would be a mark of good sense.

I look round. One is grey and scrawny, the other brown and fat, and both are hurrying towards me with a mad look in their eyes.

I am running. Only until I can think of a master plan, you understand, but these things take time.

It is extremely difficult to run with this cocktail

stick between my jaws. Of course, I am trying to picture in my mind what I should be *doing* with my weapon …

The overall image is there – lots of fancy twirling and accurate poking – but the details of how to do that are a bit sketchy …

My mind, and my heart, and my feet are racing. I can hear the rats grunting.

They're getting closer.

Stay calm.

I have no idea what I can actually do with the cocktail stick.

Just focus.

Probably nothing.

Well you either try, or you die.

I take the stick out of my mouth, hold it high in one hand, run three-legged.

'I have a cocktail stick! And I'm not afraid to use it!'

Stick is too long. Legs too short. It's going to —

— CAAATCH!! between the cobbles, POLE-VAULTING ME UP and somehow I am hanging from … a bicycle lock.

Actually, it's more of a thin chain than a proper lock, coiled loosely around handlebars and railing, and from the way I'm swinging here, I don't think it's going to hold. But here come the two rats, positioning themselves right underneath me, grinning evilly.

'I wouldn't stand there, if I were you!' In my head that was a mean threat, but it came out more as a cry of concern for their safety.

They are laughing, of course.

Ouch. My rump just bumped hard against the top of the bike, nudging it off balance. Now the silver chain is unfurling – rusted bicycle frame set free ... I squeeze my eyes shut and wait for the –

CRASH.

I open one eye and look down. The fat rat lies knocked out beneath the crumpled bicycle. Her companion stares up at me in shock.

I shrug my shoulders.

With a jerk, I drop an inch or two. My stomach turns a somersault. The tinny sound of cheap chain links running across metal railings can mean only one thing.

As the chain frees itself, it drops me in a dead-straight plummet ... and as the rat below looms closer, I meet that yellow-eyed stare, now a mix of terror and acceptance, and you know, I think we understand each other ...

There must have been a *thud*, but I don't remember feeling it. Everything has been black for a good few seconds. Perhaps I should open my eyes.

Either the world has turned blue, or I've hit my head very hard.

Actually, neither; I'm lying on my back,

looking up at the sky. I've landed on something warm and soft.

And furry and grey.

I scramble off the rat, ready with my fists. But he's been knocked out, just like his friend.

I survey the scene before me. I just took out two rats with one cocktail stick: not too bad. And to think that, for a moment there, I almost lost my nerve. But what did I tell myself? *Stay calm, and focus*. From now on I shall always remain calm and focused.

I hear a flapping of wings above me, and look up in time to see a scruffy grey pigeon take off from the top of a nearby lamp post. He is flying, I believe, in the direction of the number 32 bus route.

Clearly, my newest adventure has not gone unnoticed.

15

Rumour Has It

I have abandoned my mission.

I can tell that you're surprised. But think about it.

Clearly, I have been spied on by Francis Pigeoni, who is now heading for the alley between the Scuttled Frigate and the twenty-four-hour minimart to tell the cats of the deadly new foe who's coming their way. This means that, were I to stick to my original plan, the cats would be awaiting my arrival, making the job extremely dangerous – perhaps too dangerous, even for me. And besides, *rumours* about fearsome creatures have a habit of *exaggerating*; I'll sound *more* fearsome each time the tale is told, and the cats' fear of me will grow as Francis's story spreads through the gang.

So I slip back through the pipe, and into the mouse house.

'Hello everyone.'

'Rocco!' the mice cry, all together.

My ears are filled with cries of relief and stern lecturing from Nev's parents. Nev folds his arms and says nothing, but I can tell that he is secretly eager to hear what I've been doing. Uncle Alfie and Cousin Pip also seem mostly curious, while Tina is obviously disappointed to see me back already.

But I know how to lift the mood. After all, I've a heroic story to share. So I describe how I was chased by two rats and defeated them both using a cocktail stick, a parked bicycle and my own bodyweight.

'But Rocco,' says Tina, 'how did that stop you from going to crush the alley cats, like you said you would?'

The other mice glare at me. It may be best to tell a tiny lie.

'Well, actually, all I *really* wanted was to see for myself where they live, and maybe catch a glimpse of them. To see exactly what we're up against.'

'We're not *up against* the alley cats, Rocco,' Nev protests. 'We own the docks, and the foxes *look like* they own the docks, and that's just about enough to keep the cats *away* from the docks ... so long as we don't start appearing on *their* precious patch.'

'So why *didn't* you go there, Rocco?' asks Tina, ignoring her brother.

'Ah. Well I had to scrap that plan because the pigeon saw the whole thing. Saw what I did to the rats.'

There is silence.

'What pigeon?' says Nev's dad.

'Francis Pigeoni. He took off towards the cats' territory. Trust me – once they hear what he has to say about me, the last thing those mangy moggies will do is come anywhere near.'

Unfortunately, everyone except Tina seems to disagree. What I'm now hearing is an argument over whether the cats will mock the idea of a deadly hamster, or take the threat seriously and sneak into the docklands to take a look for themselves. I'm a little disturbed by both these theories.

'Hey Rocco.' Tina is bouncing up and down and making stabbing motions with an imaginary object. 'Show me all your moves with the cocktail stick! Did you twirl it? Did you jab it? Did you whack it?'

'Actually, I … pole-vaulted it.'

Her eyes widen in amazement. I'm beginning to feel better already.

***

It's now two days since Francis took flight in the lane, and here we all are, gathered in the chamber for one of the Big Cheese's regular rants. News travels fast, it seems, and it's not just the alley cats who've heard all about my adventures outside the Jolly Yachtsman Hotel. Yesterday two magpies were heard discussing an unusually large hamster who threw a bicycle on top of a rat, before crushing another just by jumping on him; by this morning, according to one conversation between a crow and a starling, the number of rats pounded by this fearless rodent had increased to four.

The Big Cheese chuckles down the pipe. For once, I think he is pleased with me.

'THIS TRUE THEN, IS IT, 'AMSTER? YOU REALLY ARE THE MEANEST GANGSTER ON THESE STREETS?'

'The meanest by far,' I tell him.

'SHOW NO FEAR, DO YA?'

'None whatsoever.'

'AND NO MERCY?'

I can hear the rats around me growling and exchanging angry whispers.

'Nope.'

'WELL THEN. SOUNDS LIKE EVERYONE IN TOWN KNOWS JUST HOW 'ARD WE ARE, IF THEY DIDN'T ALREADY.'

I would like to correct him by saying that they know how hard *I* am … but it might be best to say nothing.

'COME UP WIF A BETTER USE FOR THAT TALENT THAN *SELF-DEFENCE* AND I MIGHT JUST 'AVE A JOB FOR YA.'

'Thank you.'

As the meeting breaks up, I catch the wary glances of the rats as they slink from the chamber. By the looks of it, thanks to my new and fearsome reputation, no one wants to give me any trouble.

Yet for some reason, Nev is pulling me along the pipe that leads deeper into the sewer. We stop in the shafts of light beneath a drain cover.

'Rocco,' says Nev, 'you and I both know that story's been *completely* exaggerated.'

'Well, it's been embellished a little …'

'You did not throw a bicycle on someone.'

'Um, no. But I did mastermind its collapse.'

Nev looks so worried that I can't help but feel that I might still be tweaking the truth.

'All I'm saying is this: you have to keep living up to this new reputation of yours. If the rats start doubting how deadly you really are, then next time there *will* be four of them and there might *not* be a careless cyclist to save the day.'

'Don't worry about a thing,' I tell him. 'I'll live up to it no problem.'

'How?'

I'm guessing that 'By demolishing a whole load of alley cats' wouldn't be considered a sensible answer.

'I don't know. But all I have to do is step outside, and I guarantee that some proper action will happen.'

Nev opens his mouth to say something, but then hesitates. 'That certainly seems to be true.' He sighs, and I think he feels a lot better.

Now he's hugging me. If I sound surprised, that's probably because I haven't had a hug since the day I was taken away from my mother.

'You're an honorary mouse, Rocco. One of us. You're also a complete nutter, but somehow it seems to work for you. Anyway, you should know us mice stick together. We'll help you out, any way we can.'

You know, until this moment I'd thought of myself as an honorary rat. But to be one of the mice seems a very fine thing indeed, and now I come to think about it, I realise that I've felt like one of them since the minute I arrived.

'I know,' I tell him. 'And pretty soon I'll have a big say in things around here. Then things will look a lot brighter for us non-rats.'

Nev just smiles and squeezes my shoulder, and we're off again, back to the mouse house, I suppose.

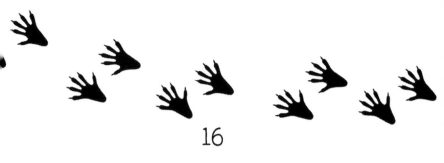

16

The Cat is Out of the Bag

As it happens, we have indeed returned to the mouse house. But perhaps not for long.

'Rocco's fierce reputation is backfiring,' says Nev's dad. 'The meanest, angriest rats know he's their biggest rival for the top job, and they're already out looking for him. And this, right here, is the first place they'll look.'

'You're right,' says Nev's mum. 'It's not safe for Rocco to stay here. In fact, it's not safe for *any* of us to stay put.'

'There's only one thing for it!' cries Tina. 'We have to declare open war!'

'Good thinking, Tina!' I tell her.

'All right. Here's an alternative plan,' says Nev, very forcefully. 'Rocco should leave, keep on the move and out of sight. We'll stay here, and when the rats come by, we'll say he's no longer our friend because we want no part in his crazy schemes. The rats are less than smart – they'll believe us and go away.'

'Then what?' asks Cousin Pip.

'Then … we'll put a scrap of white napkin by the bins behind Chef Claude's. Rocco, when you see that, you'll know it's safe to come back. Although you mustn't be seen with us mice again, or they'll know we lied.'

'Agreed!' I reply. 'I'll sneak out of here, and keep well out of sight!'

That didn't sound nearly as daring as I'd have liked.

I am wandering around the streets, diving for cover each time I suspect there is a rat nearby. Not because I am not fearless, but because I am following Nev's plan, and anyway, I prefer to spare their lives.

It would be wise, then, to stick to the backstreets. I run up the nearest one, and hide under a parked car. It's cool and shady under here … but a fat drop of motor oil on the head is enough to make me lose my patience. I need to do *something*. Something major. Something that will add to my reputation for fearsomeness, or courageousness, or general awesomeness. But what? I'll just have to keep hanging around until I hit on a brilliant idea …

There's a tapping on the cobbles up ahead. It's faint, but unmistakeable: the sound of someone with large, clawed toes running across the street.

I peek out from under my parked car just in time to see a monstrous shadow looming on the wall at the end of the street. It is the shadow of someone with gaping jaws and jagged teeth, huge pointed ears and a bushy tail ... Wait a minute, a bushy tail surely means ... Yes – there he is: it's a fox. But it can't be one of *our* foxes, I mean this guy is not to be messed with.

Actually ...

Is that *Maurice*?

I remember what Nev said about the foxes being experts at acting fierce, and I must say I'm impressed. Maurice has slunk out of sight. Perhaps I'll go after him, see where he's off to ...

I stop dead, because it seems that our canine client is not alone. The shadow of a smaller animal is darkening the wall – someone low and sleek. I can hear a van rumbling along the road, so I duck behind the front wheel of my parked car. As soon as the van's gone past I hurry straight out again, but the fox's companion has slipped from my sight.

So now I'm running to catch up. At the end of the street I round the corner at such speed that for a moment my back feet swing right out past my front ones. I tear across the road, and leap over the kerb … and press my back to the wall and stay very still, because … okay, because I really have to catch my breath, but also … I saw enough cartoons on Gary's TV … to know that this is the proper way to *spy*.

I'm just in time to see that bushy tail disappearing down the lane that leads to the foxes' yard. Maurice's mysterious acquaintance must have entered the lane first. I follow – tiptoeing at first, because that's what spies do. But on the other hand, I'm small, which means I'm quiet even when I'm running, and also means that for me the lane is quite far away.

So now I'm running again, as fast as I can.

I pause, peering into the lane. It is very dark, despite the broad daylight. So this time it really is best to tiptoe.

As I move along the lane I can hear voices. I can't make out what they're saying, so I tiptoe faster. Just ahead, the wall on the left has partly collapsed, allowing open access to the foxes' yard on the other side. I scramble over a pile of broken bricks and peer cautiously through the gap.

Maurice is sitting calmly in the middle of the yard, licking his paw. But where is his slippery friend?

I can see movement inside the doorway of the nearest shed.

'So what do you think?' asks Maurice. 'You've seen everything now.'

'I most certainly have,' replies a voice from the doorway, cool and aloof but definitely impressed.

'Well then,' says Maurice, 'shall we be doing business?'

'Oh, I think so.'

The speaker steps out of the shed. I see pale fur, pointed ears, eyes gleaming with murderous intent. *I see a cat.*

But no fluffy, pampered pet like my former housemate; oh no, this is a scrawny, mean-faced feline, face and tail black with dirt. She has bigger plans than attacking hamsters in plastic balls. I can't breathe.

This is an alley cat.

'It's perfectly simple,' Maurice is saying. 'You bring your payment, as discussed, and all of this is yours.'

'I'll look forward to it,' purrs the cat. 'As shall all the other members of my *social circle*.'

I can't believe it. The alley cats are coming. They're taking over the docklands. The foxes are *selling* their patch to them.

It's a betrayal. And it's about to become a war.

'You know what we cats have to deal with. All this trouble over some ridiculous hyperactive hamster. I'll soon take care of *that*, but it will be nice to do so after a well-earned rest and some *delicious* refreshments.'

Maurice is saying something, but his voice is nothing but a dull echo in my head. I feel dizzy. The mice – some of them at least – suggested something like this might happen. Am I giddy with alarm, or excitement? I'm going to say *excitement*, and I'll tell you why: because I swear that this is it. This is my chance to *shine* exactly as the Big Cheese wants me to.

The evil meeting seems to be at an end. Maurice slinks into the furthest shed, and the cat – that smug, plotting, skin-and-bones alley cat – slips from the yard.

I run as fast as any hamster can, all the way to the sewer, almost skidding as I pass behind Chef Claude's on a white rag that was supposed to bring me back home to the mice, but I can't go to the mouse house right now.

17

Visiting Old Friends is More Dangerous Than You'd Think

The rats have stopped looking like they're about to kill me. Instead, they appear panic-stricken. Even the Big Cheese has gone quiet.

'SO … YOU MEAN THE ALLEY CATS ARE MOVIN' IN?'

'Yes.'

'TO ENJOY THE FINE CUISINE, OR TO KILL THE HYPERACTIVE 'AMSTER?'

'Both, I think. In that order.' This feels like a very proud moment. 'News of my deeds has reached the alley cats,' I declare. 'They feel threatened and their pride is hurt: we, the rodents, are the most feared gang of all.'

Murmurs of agreement from the crowd.

'Their desire is to sneak into these docklands, destroy us, and take all the glory. Not to mention the food: let me tell you, no scrap is safe.'

Cries of alarm and outrage.

'Of course, they know now something of the foxes' true nature – Maurice was his usual well-mannered self. But those foxes are cunning animals. I'll bet they're letting those cats believe they really *do* have a murderous side that'll soon shine through if the cats try anything clever. Because these kitties are not so big; in fact, the one I saw was puny and thin. That's why, rather than risk a fight, they have offered the foxes some kind of payment they cannot refuse, in exchange for their territory.'

A cloud of fear and fury hangs over the chamber. Puny and thin as the cats may be, it now seems that they're also rather smart.

'I ALWAYS KNEW THOSE FOXES WAS NOTHIN' BUT TROUBLE.'

I hope that's not all the Big Cheese is going to say. Everyone looks uncomfortable, waiting for the boss rat to announce his plan of action. I risk looking around for my friends. I can see Nev up the back of the room. And Tina, already practising her karate chops.

'So what do we do?' someone shouts at last.

'We need more facts,' says a small rat near the back. 'We need to know *exactly* what them cats is up to, and when they're plannin' on comin'.'

'WE NEED MORE FACTS.'

'You mean someone should go see the mole?' asks another voice.

'I MEAN SOMEONE SHOULD GO SEE THE MOLE.'

They must mean my good friend, Dwayne. It would be so much fun meeting him again.

'I'll go,' I say.

'ALL RIGHT THEN. THE 'AMSTER WILL GO SEE OUR MOLE AND FIND OUT WHAT HE KNOWS.'

'Absolutely. I'll find out what he knows.'

'AND 'OO ARE YOU TAKIN' WITH YOU?'

'Actually, I'm quite happy to work alone.'

A rat standing near me shakes his head and draws a finger across his throat.

'NO CAN DO. YOU GO SEE THE MOLE IN PAIRS. IN CASE ONE OF YOU GETS POUNCED ON BY AN UNFRIENDLY GANG, OR EATEN ON THE WAY BACK.'

'Eaten?'

'THEM'S THE RULES. SO 'OO'S IT GONNA BE?'

'*I'll* go with Rocco,' shouts Nev. 'A white-and-gold hamster sticks out so badly that he might as well wear a target on his back. Especially one who's made such a *name* for himself. So you want someone small and hard to spot going with him.'

I don't feel hurt by this, because you must

remember that Nev is playing the part of someone who no longer wishes to be my friend.

'THAT FIGURES. IT'S SORTED THEN. THE 'AMSTER AND THE MOUSE WILL GO SEE THE MOLE TONIGHT.'

We're back in the mouse house. Nev's parents, Uncle Alfie and even Cousin Pip are in a gloomy mood. Nev looks as though he's thinking very hard.

'Nev,' I say, 'I want to thank you for coming with me. I know it must seem like my courage is endless, but I do know that this could get dangerous.'

'It's like I said,' he replies. 'Us mice stick together. I couldn't let you go with any of those rats, could I?'

'You know,' says Nev's dad, 'it's true that we small folk stay out of trouble as much as possible. But going looking for danger, and facing up to it when it comes knocking, well those are two different things. And we face danger head-on most days of our lives.'

'And besides' – Nev points towards the wall with his thumb – 'you don't have a whole lot of choice, when you're trying to hold on to someone who's wriggling like crazy, and you've got your hand over their mouth, except they're biting it like they're trying to draw blood ...'

Until now I hadn't really noticed Tina, lying curled up in the shadows. Without getting up, she turns herself around to face the wall. I realise now that she wanted to come with me, and tried to say so back in the chamber.

I feel sad for her. I'd go over and cheer her up … if only I knew how …

'So Nev,' I say quickly, 'you're the expert on visits to Dwayne. I'll leave it to you to decide when we should begin our mission.'

'Well, the foxes that live around the park only come out late at night … There are other rodent gangs, of course, and pet cats, but you can come across them any time. The biggest threat will be the owls in the park. But again, they usually come out late. So the best time is probably sunset, just as it gets dark.'

Something he just said has given me a queasy feeling.

'Did you say *owls*?'

'I sure did. You remember what the Big Cheese said about being eaten?'

Owls: silent assassins of the night. I'd mop the floor with their feathered faces, of course, but it's rather difficult to hear them coming.

'That's settled then,' I declare. 'We leave at sunset.'

18

I, Spy

It's been a cloudy evening, and now, as the sun goes down, it's already pretty dark. Nev says that's a good thing. He's stealing along the pavement like a secret agent whose cover's just been blown, and I'm making sure to do likewise.

It turns out that I went the long way when I surfed downtown through the drainage system. In fact the docklands are not far from Dwayne's park; not when you're running like we are, at least. Nev's tail and the soles of his feet are all that I can see in front of me. He's light and speedy and it's a bit of a struggle trying to keep up. We're running under hedges or close in against railings, pausing from time to time to hide from passing pedestrians.

Nev stops suddenly, and I almost run right into him. He is pointing at something across the street.

I recognise the park gates immediately, although it's almost completely dark now and the orange street lights are just warming up. To my surprise, I am already alone on the pavement. Nev has sprung on to the road and, in an instant, has almost reached the other side. I can just about make out his small grey figure as he jumps on to the kerb opposite. He turns around.

'*Rocco!*' he hisses. '*Why are you still standing there?*'

'*Sorry!*' I whisper back.

I leap on to the road. As my feet hit the tarmac, I am suddenly aware of a pair of bright lights, coming towards me fast.

'NOT NOW!!!' yells Nev.

I lie flat. My hands are over my head. *Mustn't move.* An engine roars loud. *Mustn't die.* I open one eye: blinding white light … now pitch black.

Am I dead?

Well, the street lights are back … the engine is fading into the distance … and Nev is shouting.

'Get up, Rocco, you crazy hamster! Get over here now!' It seems I have curled myself into the tightest of balls. I untangle my limbs and hurry across the road. 'For a second there I thought you were *dead.*'

'Actually, that was carefully timed so I'd land in that exact spot just as the car passed over.'

Nev gives me an exasperated look that quickly

dissolves into relief. 'Come on then,' he says, 'let's go see the mole.'

We turn towards the gates. It's dark in the park; the way through is marked by a few splashes of white light from the lamps lining the path.

'We stick close together,' says Nev. 'I'll scan around and behind us, you keep a watch on the sky. You ready?'

'Of course,' I reply. I guess this means I'm looking out for owls.

We walk through the gates. I hear a rustling sound behind us. Or did I? I might have imagined it, but I'd swear Nev is suddenly moving more slowly, more softly.

There it is again. We stop. We look at each other. As one, we turn around, looking this way and that while slowly walking backwards, deeper into the park.

And again! Closer this time – coming from the bushes to our right.

Whoa! Something shoots out of the undergrowth – darts on to the dimly lit path – straight towards Nev!

It smacks into him, bowls him over.

'AAAAAHHH!' he cries.

Mind you … Nev's attacker is very small, and familiar, and is wearing a pink shoelace around her head.

'Nev ...'

He is still yelling.

'It's all right, Nev. It's only Tina.'

Nev stares at his little sister in shock. Tina rolls on to the ground, laughing.

'*Tina!*' Nev scrambles to his feet. He looks ready to explode. 'No! This cannot be happening! You can't be here, Tina, you just can't!'

Now it's Tina's turn to look annoyed. 'Yes I can! I'm a way better spy than you are! I followed you here, didn't I, and you didn't even know I was there!'

Nev groans. 'This isn't a *game*, Tina. You're not old enough to come on these trips. Mum and Dad will be worried sick ...'

'You're not sending me home!'

'Too right, I'm not sending you home. It's far too dangerous for you to go back alone at this time of night.'

Perhaps that was a kind of mind trick, designed to make Tina *want* to turn around and go home, just to prove she can. If it was, it didn't work. She folds her arms and glares.

'Okay,' says Nev, 'how about this: why don't you stay here, and keep a lookout? Now *that's* an important job.'

Tina considers this. 'Looking out for foes?'

'Exactly.'

'I'll be the first to see 'em coming.'

'Our lives will be in your hands.'

Tina looks thoughtful. 'All right then,' she says importantly. 'I'll do it.'

'Look over here,' I tell the others. I drag a large empty sweetie packet from under a bush. 'If you hide in this, Tina, you can stay on the path and get a much better view than you'd get from the bushes.'

Tina crawls inside the packet. She looks out at us through the clear window in the front, and grins. 'I can see *everything*!' she exclaims in a muffled voice.

Somehow I doubt that she can, since the window is rather small, and smeared with sticky sugar.

'Excellent,' says Nev.

And so we leave Tina in a sweetie bag by the gates, and slip silently across the grass. I don't see why she can't join in, but then, Nev is only trying to protect his little sister …

I have a sudden, strange feeling – a distant memory of my smallest brother, I think. That's right: he fell off the hamster wheel and I ran straight over, worried he might be hurt …

I give myself a shake, and the memory's gone. I have to concentrate on the here and now, because this is it: we're running through open space, with no cover for miles around. My heart is thudding with excitement. I can't see very much in the dark, but Nev has made this journey many times and seems to know exactly where to go.

'Here we are,' he says.

We stop beside the same molehill that Dwayne popped out of the last time we met. Nev picks up a pebble that was half-buried in the mound, moves a few feet away, and hurls the stone at the molehill.

It lands with a soft *smack* and sets off a tiny landslide.

'Give him ten seconds,' says Nev.

I count in my head ... five, six, seven, eight ... Already the soil is flying – and now up pops Dwayne: pink hands, followed by pink nose, followed by black fuzzy head.

The pink nose sniffs.

'Nev?' asks Dwayne. 'Is that you?'

'It is me, and a friend of mine who I think you've met before.'

The nose sniffs again, then suddenly stops. 'It can't be ...'

'Hello Dwayne!' I say. 'It's me, Rocco. It's so great to see you again. I joined the gang, as you can tell.'

'Er ... yes. That's good, I suppose.'

'Can we come in, Dwayne?' Nev glances around nervously. 'It's feeling a bit, you know ... chilly out here.'

'Oh yes, of course.'

Dwayne disappears into the molehill, and we quickly follow. It's pitch dark down here.

'Come in here,' says Dwayne, nudging us into what feels like a small chamber.

'Thanks Dwayne,' says Nev. 'We'll keep this as short as possible, because my sister's in a sweetie packet out by the gates.'

'Oh.'

'I guess you know why we're here, anyway, so just fire ahead. Tell us whatever you know.'

Of course, I can't make out Dwayne's face in the dark – but somehow his silence speaks volumes.

'No,' he says. 'I'm afraid I *don't* know.'

'It's the alley cats,' I say helpfully. 'We need to know everything you've got on the deal they're doing with the foxes down at the docks.'

'That's right,' adds Nev. 'Everything on when they're moving in, and what they plan to do next.'

Despite the darkness – not to mention his blindness – I sense that Dwayne is really staring at us.

'I've no idea what you're talking about.'

'We're talking about how the alley cats are buying the foxes' patch,' I tell him, 'so that they can take over the docks.'

As you'll remember, the last time I was here I learned that you do have to prod Dwayne for information.

'Do you have *anything* on the alley cats?' asks Nev. He's beginning to sound worried.

'Well, no,' says Dwayne, and now there's real panic in his voice, 'not since they tried to hijack Lou's fresh fish van on its way to Chef Claude's. That was three weeks ago.'

'You see, Rocco overheard a conversation between one of the cats and one of the foxes.'

'Plotting our downfall,' I chip in, because this conversation is not proving as exciting as I had hoped.

'Well you know a lot more than me, I'm afraid,' says Dwayne. 'Oh, gosh – I've been trying *so* hard to spy on them, I really have, but it just seemed like they weren't *doing* anything.'

Nev sighs. 'This isn't good,' he says. 'They're crafty, if they can keep a plan as big as this one completely spy-proof.'

'I'm sorry.'

'That's all right, Dwayne. It's not your fault.' I can hear Nev shuffling back into the tunnel. 'We better get back up there and collect my little sister, before it gets any later.'

We're heading back towards the molehill.

'Please!' wails Dwayne. 'Tell the Big Cheese I've tried my best!'

'Of course we will,' says Nev. 'Don't you worry.' But I know Nev is just as worried as the mole.

We scramble back up to the surface. As we pull ourselves out of the soil, I am suddenly aware of something square-shaped running headlong towards us.

'What's that?' I ask, squinting through the darkness.

'AAAHH!' replies Nev. 'What the — ?!'

Together we start scrabbling back into the earth, but Dwayne has been coming up right behind us and is screaming for us to stop.

I turn around. I could swear that the running square just let out a muffled yell of its own. And at last I can make out the words FIZZTASTIC FEAST across its front.

'It's Tina!' I shout.

'Tina?' Nev half-tumbles off the molehill. 'Tina, what's the matter?'

'OOWWW!' exclaims Tina from inside the packet.

'What did you say? Are you hurt?' screams Nev. Together, we lift the bag clear of her head.

'NO!!!' comes the reply. She points up – or behind – it's difficult to say where. 'I *said* there's an OWL!!'

'OWL!' shrieks Dwayne, diving back into the tunnel.

Nev, Tina and I grab each other in a three-way hug, dropping the bag over ourselves.

'*Where?*' whispers Nev.

'I don't know where he is now,' says Tina, annoyed. 'I had to run all the way over here to tell you, because that's my job, and now he could be anywhere.'

It's a bit crowded with three of us in this bag. We're breathing hard, and it's already getting hot and rather syrupy.

'I suppose we'd better stay in the packet,' I say, reluctantly, 'and try to make our way back to the gates.'

'Rocco's right,' agrees Nev. 'We'll take it slowly. Everyone just keep both eyes on the sky.'

We begin shuffling our way across the park, stepping on each other's toes. The bag is sticking to me back and front. And worst of all, the window in the front of the packet is now completely covered in a gloopy mix of hot breath and sugar.

'I don't think we're moving in a straight line,' I say. 'Maybe we should stop and get our bearings.'

We stop.

'We need to take the bag off for a moment,' I say.

'How's about this,' says Nev. 'We take it off, I'll look for the gates, Tina can watch the sky ahead and to the left of us, and Rocco can look out behind and to the right. We all count to three, then the bag goes back on. Agreed?'

'Agreed!' say Tina and I together.

We slide the slick packet over our heads. I gasp in the fresh air and feel completely lost. Clearly,

I'm not the only one who's confused, because rather than scanning our patches of sky, Tina and I are staring straight at one another.

'*One ...*' says Nev slowly. He screws up his eyes as he peers through the darkness.

I look up.

'*... two ...*'

I hear something. It's ... a flapping sound ... like wings!

'THREE, THREE, THREE!!' screams Tina.

We snatch up the packet and lift it over our heads. The plastic crinkles as we all pull it in different directions.

I'd swear I just felt it tear.

'AAAAHHHHH!!!'

We're under attack! Oh, you must be kidding me – a pair of *clawed feet* are pressing down on us through the packet.

'THE PATH IS THAT WAY!!' yells Nev.

WHAT WAY??!! Somehow we're all running in the same direction. But I can feel that tear widening, and—

AAAH! One of those claws, tickling my side!

Just run, Rocco. And breathe. Run and—

—breathe!

The rush of cool night air can only mean one thing:

'PACKET'S GONE!!' I cry.

We stop running, grab hold of each other,

look up. Our attacker is flying away, carrying the sweetie bag, lost already in the darkness …

'He thinks he's got us!' whispers Nev.

But hang on … isn't that the packet, fluttering back to earth?

I can make out the outline of beating wings … circling around … *heading straight for us.*

'Not any more, he doesn't!' I hiss.

'Take cover!' cries Tina, and we all dive forward. I glance up – the owl is plunging through the air.

Don't. Get. Eaten.

We leap.

Snatch up the precious slip of plastic.

Run.

Holding the bag over our heads now, and oh, *help, the claws are back*, and the deafening beat of those wings, right in my ears.

But now it's suddenly gone quiet. I'll bet the winged villain is flying up nice and high, preparing for a killer dive.

'TREES AT TWO O'CLOCK!!' hollers Nev.

'TREES WHEN?' I ask.

'CRASH 'N' BURN BIRDIE!' declares Tina.

I lift my corner of the sweetie packet, just enough to glance at what lies ahead. I see the trees – and I get the idea.

'KEEP GOING STRAIGHT!' I shout. 'TILL THE VERY LAST MINUTE!'

We run faster than ever …

Ignore the wing noise …

But it's coming back fast.

A tree root looms ahead. We swerve suddenly to the right —

And are followed.

OOMPH.

That is the sound of an owl in flight smacking into a tree trunk.

'Bullseye!' says Tina.

He's dazed, no doubt. But we're not hanging around to find out. Of course, I could do with getting my breath back, but … too risky to stand still …

So we keep running.

Grass is more worn here. Bit muddy.

Think that means we're near the —

— *path.* We all stumble as we hit the tarmac, but by now we're even *tripping* in perfect harmony. We sprint across its smooth surface —

'Ow!' says Nev.

We're lying in a prickly bush. Everyone is gasping for air. Should we move? Maybe someone should move, take a look outside the bush. Tina's peering out through the tangle of spiky little branches.

'It's the gates!' she says.

Nev and I pull each other to our feet.

'Any sign of you-know-who?' asks Nev.

'Negative!'

We drag the sweetie bag clear of the bush. You can't be too careful in warfare, so we pull it back over our heads and tiptoe towards the gates.

And so at last we reach the street.

We lift off the bag, toss it aside. Nev looks up at the bright street light overhead. 'You know,' he says, 'it might not be a bad idea to keep ourselves under cover.'

Enough said. I think we're all feeling a little too visible right now. So it's back on with the bag, and off we go.

19

A Business Proposal

Let's just say the rats are deeply unhappy about the news of the alley cats' secrecy. Like Dwayne himself, Nev and I feared that the Big Cheese might be furious with our clueless mole, but he's too busy getting angry about the foxes' betrayal.

'GOOD HONEST BUSINESS RATS, THAT'S ALL WE'VE EVER BEEN TO THEM. NEVER LET THOSE GULLS PINCH A THING. AND THIS IS HOW THEY PAY US BACK. WELL THE FINAL PAYBACK WILL BE OURS, AND NO MISTAKE.'

What does he mean by *that*, you ask?

Let me bring you up to speed. We have just learned that the gang would now like to collect a bigger variety of awesome deadly weapons: a whole new range. Not because an all-out feud with the foxes is likely; after all, those foxes can't handle themselves in a fight. No, the idea is to threaten them until they promise to call off their deal with the cats. I'm sure that a few stern words will do the trick, but the new weapons will be good to have, just for effect. Of course, it's possible the cats will still attack, all in a rage over the deal falling through, or seeing at last that the foxes aren't capable of being dangerous. And that's when the new weaponry will be essential.

All right, so the rats are very specific about the type of weapons we'll be collecting. They must be sharp. They are also likely to be shiny, because we're going to get them from an arms trading deal with a gang of magpies.

'THAT'S ONE THING I'LL SAY FOR THEM MAGPIES,' the Big Cheese is saying, 'THEY'RE NEVER SHORT ON THINGS WHAT ARE SHARP AND THINGS WHAT ARE SHINY.'

I'm not sure why shiny is an advantage, but it's certainly going down well with the crowd. I think the Big Cheese is beginning to enjoy himself; he seems very excited about what he calls *an unscheduled business meeting in the foxes' yard.* 'AND THEM FOXES BETTER DO AS THEY'RE TOLD,' he assures us, 'OR IT'S CURTAINS FOR THEM *AND* THEIR MOGGY MATES. NOW. SOMEONE GO SET UP AN APPOINTMENT WITH THE MAGPIES.'

Four rats group together and run from the chamber.

'AND ONE MORE THING. IT MIGHT BE BEST IF THE 'AMSTER TAGS ALONG WHEN YOU DO THE DEAL. HE SEEMS TO BE 'ANDY IN A TIGHT SPOT.'

I can feel a warm glow inside me.

Back at the mouse house, the mice, as usual, are less enthusiastic. I don't quite understand why; after all, my next outing with the rats is only to carry out a simple business deal.

Tina, of course, is disappointed *not* to be going.

'Don't worry, Tina – you won't miss anything,' I tell her. 'The magpies know all about my fearsome reputation. My being there will put them off trying any funny business.'

This seems to cheer her up, and I think she's okay about being left behind. After all, a proper fight might just be coming – rodents versus cats – and if it does come she'll have plenty opportunities to shine as a martial arts warrior.

It's time for bed, so I hop into the matchbox where I sleep, right next to Nev's.

'You know, Rocco,' says Nev, 'sometimes these things get sticky. There's no shame whatsoever in just keeping out of sight.'

Sometimes I rather suspect that he's missing the point.

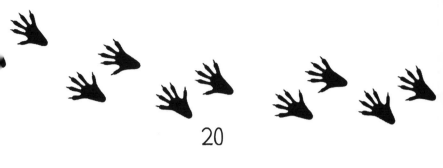

20

Trick or Treat

We're ready to go. The weapons spread out before me are like nothing I've ever seen. There are pizza wheels, fish slices, wooden spoons. This is the life I've been dreaming of.

Naturally, the idea behind tonight's meeting is that we will take one or two of each kind of weapon, and swap them for whatever it is that the magpies have to offer. Now the mice have told me, many times, to keep quiet in the company of the rats, but right now I'm much too excited to do that. Besides, I am Rocco the Infamous, most powerful rodent on this trip and all-round star of the show.

'Shall we be giving the magpies one of everything?' I ask.

From the long silence, I'd say the answer is

most likely *no*. I think someone at the back of the room just gave a chuckle. Yes, they did, because now *everyone's* laughing. A large chubby rat gives me a slap on the back that nearly knocks me flat.

'Okay, enough jokes,' declares Vinny. You might remember Vinny, the rat who tried to take over when Minestroni died. 'Let's have the goodies out here, see what we've got to bargain with.'

Clearly, he has taken charge – which is rather annoying, actually, as I'd been planning to take on the leadership role myself ... even if I'm not entirely clued up on what we're actually doing. That said, although there are a few grumblings about Vinny's power-snatching, there's hardly the furious disagreement you'd expect. It seems that no other rat wants to take the lead tonight; like everyone's super keen on the *idea* of snaffling the magpies' weapons, but without having to *deal* with the magpies themselves.

The crowd parts to let two rats pass through. They are walking backwards, dragging a large cloth napkin. The napkin is laden with silverware that you'd find in any kitchen. There are teaspoons, and salt and pepper pots, and napkin rings. But mostly teaspoons.

Nobody is saying anything. Someone really should, so I'll try this:

'Well that's the shiniest load of stolen goods *I've* ever seen.'

'Exactly!' Vinny looks delighted, and slightly crazy. 'And don't them magpies just love shiny! They'll go daft over this lot, give us all the sharp stuff they've got.'

Everyone is exchanging surprised glances. A cautious murmur of agreement quickly spreads and becomes a rumble of enthusiasm. But I don't quite understand why. I mean, is *shiny* really enough? Won't the magpies want some of *our* dangerous weapons, in exchange for theirs? Are teaspoons and salt pots dangerous? Am I missing something here?

Anyway, it looks like we're off. The napkin is swiftly folded and tied at the corners to make a bundle, and the same two rats start dragging it away. We all follow, and now there is a real sense of excitement in the air. But for some reason, I don't seem to be sharing that excitement. In fact, suddenly I have a bit of a headache. Maybe I've been down in the sewer too long.

I'm glad to see the light from street lamps at the end of the tunnel. The mice are waiting there to see us off.

'Cheerio,' I tell them.

Nev pulls me aside. 'Just remember what I said, Rocco. About staying out of sight.'

Tina gives me a high five.

I'm glad it wasn't far to the cake factory where the meeting is to take place. I can't help feeling that this many rats (and one hamster), out and about with a large bundle of silverware, could attract some unwanted attention. Of course, that's why we're doing this at three a.m.: this is gang business, and gang business is secret business.

We cross the yard in front of the cake factory. A basement window has been jammed open with a brick. Vinny slips through it, and the others follow. I am the famous, fearless Hamster Gangster, so I really should be among the first to go inside. Being smaller, I easily dart through the window alongside two of the rats.

The factory basement is in darkness, but large squares of yellow light are falling in through the row of high windows. Having dropped on to a shelf laden with bags of – wait till my eyes adjust – caster sugar, I can see that it's quite a long way to the floor. To my left and right, the rats are sinking their claws into the wooden posts at either end of the shelving unit. There is an unpleasant scratching sound as they descend to the floor.

I scurry to the post on my right and wait my turn. Rather cleverly, I think, I find the holes left by the rats' claws where they stuck them into the wood. I slot my own fingers into the holes and swing myself off the shelf … Okay, now I just have to slowly release my grasp until I start to …

slide, and … oh, here we *gooooOOOHHH*!

Ow. It's okay. I'm okay. Claws aren't as long as the rats', so … came unstuck, that's all.

I can hear someone tearing down the post above me, so I roll quickly out of the way and on to my feet. I look around, but all I can make out are the packets, tins and bottles of ingredients on the shadowy shelves. It seems we're the first to arrive – but then, isn't that the glimmer of two beady eyes, staring out from between those bags of self-raising flour?

As the last of our gang reaches the floor, there is a deadly silence. Vinny scurries into the centre of the room and stands on his hind legs.

'All right then, Joe and Co.,' he says loudly. 'We're here and we're ready to do business.'

Suddenly there are many more pairs of beady eyes, and a good deal of flapping and fluttering and whipping up a cloud of dust and flour as the magpies come down from the shelves.

They are carrying things. Jostling each other with their beating wings, they set these things down on the floor. There are pins and needles, letter openers and silver nail files. This stuff is unmistakeably shiny and impressively sharp.

'Okay,' says the biggest of the magpies (let's assume this is Joe). 'So what have you got for *us*, Vinny?'

All of us are looking around … looking for

the two rats who hauled the napkin stuffed with goodies.

Except they're not actually here.

There is a loud clattering above us: here they come. Together with the bundle, they've just dropped through the window and on to the caster sugar shelf.

Panting, they heave the loot to the end of the shelf … Now one is positioning himself on the wooden post, pulling the bundle towards him. It's over his head and he's reaching up with one hand, trying to support its weight … The other is holding the napkin where it's tied at the top … and as the first rat slides just a little way down the post, the second fixes himself to it higher up.

The second rat is coming down … too quickly! The first looks like he's being swallowed up by the bundle as it drops on top of him. Can he hold on?

No. He's lost his grip on the post but not the napkin … he's hanging there, but … ah, yes. Too much weight for Rat Number Two.

CRASH.

All of us are cringing. At last Vinny storms over and hauls the napkin off the dazed rats. He unties the knot, revealing the silverware. The magpies stare. I feel that I should use my reputation to make sure they don't mess with us, so I shuffle closer to Vinny and the napkin. But not too close.

Somehow I want to scare the magpies with my presence, and also remain unseen.

Joe cocks his head to one side. 'What's this exactly?'

'What does it look like?' says Vinny. 'It's only the finest shiny stuff from the best restaurants in this city.'

'And what are we supposed to do with a load of teaspoons? You lot tryin' to *stir* up a fight?'

The other birds caw with laughter.

'Nice try Joey,' says Vinny. 'We all know you birdbrains go crackers for the likes of them teaspoons. I guess you can see your reflection real good in them, for preening all them fancy-pants feathers.'

There is a dangerous gleam in Joe's eye. 'Don't push it! You ain't the only gang here lookin' for weaponry. So you see, this stuff ain't no use to us – unless our enemies are gonna *sneeze* to death …'

Joe kicks over a little silver pepper pot, sending a plume of brown powder into the air. The rats gasp at such a waste of seasoning.

The magpies move forward, closing in on us.

'We 'ave a hamster,' shouts Vinny, 'and we're not afraid to use him!'

'That's right!' I squeak, although I really didn't mean to. I clap my hands firmly over my mouth.

Everyone is looking at me. Quickly, I drop my hands, clenching my fists – then I stretch up on my hind legs, making myself as tall as possible ...

And as I'm doing so, it's making me think. I *knew* all that harmless kitchenware would not impress the magpies; I *knew* trouble was brewing. I am super smart. The magpies may be many, and big, and their beaks may be sharp – but they're not half as sharp as Rocco the Quick-witted.

So why are they giggling?

'Oh, of course, how could we forget?' says Joe. 'Maybe it's 'cause he's not quite the two-foot-tall, bike-flingin' freak of nature all the rumours was describin'?'

Now the magpies are almost helpless with laughter. Vinny looks at me and seems to be panicking.

As for me – I'm ready to teach this beaky buffoon a thing or two.

'You think size is everything?' I yell.

'Let's find out!' says Joe. 'We fight for the sharp stuff!'

Everyone takes a flying leap at the weaponry offered up by the magpies. I run in among them, but already everything has gone. So I grab one of our teaspoons instead.

The air is filled with the tuneful ringing of silver things striking other silver things. Suddenly a large bird is right in my face. I smack him across the beak with the back of my spoon.

'SQUAWK!'

He backs off.

And here's another! I give him the same.

'Ah-ha!' I cry. 'Perhaps you *should* believe the rumours!'

The first magpie lifts his right foot. In it he is clutching a long needle.

He jabs – I hop to the left. He jabs again – I hop to the right. I swing my spoon and wallop him on the head. His eyes cross as he keels over.

'I JUST KNOCKED OUT A MAGPIE!'

I couldn't help remarking on that, but it seems to have made the second fellow rather angry. He has a nail file. I spring backwards as he swipes it at me —

'Aaahh!'

— Not quite – *ow* – fast enough to avoid getting my – *geez, that smarts* – nose filed. I grab the rounded end of my spoon and poke him hard in the belly with the handle. He flaps across the room muttering things I will not repeat.

'Two down! Who's next?'

That'll be the huge bird standing right behind me, grasping a letter opener like a dagger in her long claws.

She takes a stab at me. I block it with my spoon – and just like that, it's a sword fight! She raises the blade high – I lift my spoon up – she brings it down, pokes it at my middle – I smack it clean away!

You may not think a teaspoon seems a natural substitute for a sword, but actually it works extremely well —

Ah. Until it's knocked out of your hands.

The magpie lunges – but I'm already out of there, bolting past her. She spins around, looking for me. But she can't see me, because I'm underneath a shelving unit, hard against the wall.

She's walking towards me. She still can't see me – it's too dark – but she will, once she's close enough. Can she fit herself under this shelf?

I don't know. And why should I care? She's clearly evil, and good will always triumph over evil. It just has to figure out how.

Or maybe it doesn't. My feathered foe has been pounced on by a rat with a salt pot – and it seems that seasoning in the eye works even better than a teaspoon in the gut, because she's just taken flight and slammed into the wall. It looks like our shiny loot is more useful than anyone imagined.

The question is: what do I do now? I can't see much from under here, which makes thinking up a genius plan especially difficult. Nev's last words to me are flashing through my mind: *Just remember what I said*. I do remember. He told me that there's no shame in staying out of sight, and at last I think I understand what he meant. He meant: keep yourself hidden while you find the ideal spot from which to take the enemy by surprise.

Good plan, Nev!

I move to the end of the shelving unit. Happily, there's a doorway here, meaning no neighbouring shelves. And so I begin scrambling my way up: grasping the end of a shelf ... climbing on top of the ingredients stacked there ... reaching up to grab the shelf above ...

Well, all of that is harder than it sounds. But – wow! – the view from up here is –

– terrible, actually. Everyone is hitting and prodding each other with items that birds and rodents were not designed to use, and neither side is making any progress. It is now clear that I alone can lead us to victory. I must think fast.

I look around. I see tins and packets: condensed milk, treacle, brown sugar. I need something more deadly! But there is nothing deadly here on the top shelf.

Just condensed milk ... and treacle ... and brown sugar.

Treacle ...

Are you thinking what I'm thinking? Because I'm remembering something else Nev said. He said, *Sometimes these things get sticky.*

Of course! These are not ingredients. They are *weapons*. I climb on top of the nearest treacle tin. Now I'm prising off the lid. Very slowly, because ... it's a pretty tight fit, of course, but ... here it comes ...

POP.

Suddenly I'm lying on my back on the shelf, holding the lid in both hands. I stand up, holding on to the tin and peering over the rim. The stuff inside is thick and black, and smells sickeningly sweet. I look around the room: the rats and magpies are spread out across the floor. That won't do.

I take a deep breath. There's nothing else for it.

'Attention, everyone!' I yell. 'This fight is over! The rats have won!' Everyone stops and looks up, glancing around in confusion until they spot me on my shelf. 'They have a secret weapon – and it's right up here, with me! You doubt me, you magpies, because I am not tall! And yet you stand there on the floor rather than challenge me! Well, you've got five seconds before things get nasty!'

It's working. The magpies look furious, the whole lot of them are hopping in my direction. They're spreading their wings – about to fly up here …

Time to tip the tin! I push it on to its side … and yes, the treacle is pouring down, but by golly, it's thick! *Pour faster!!*

And there you go! The first couple of magpies to get a coating of the sticky stuff squawk in horror, stopping the other birds in their tracks. Giving me time for a genius move!

I'm on top of the tin. Running on the spot, like

I used to do on my hamster wheel back at Gary's place. Except this time, I'm *moving* – backwards – spreading the trickle of treacle along the line of astonished magpies! They're yelling all sorts, flapping their wings and jumping around like crazy, but that's only helping to spread the stuff far and wide.

I jump round to face the other way – land perfectly on top of the tin – now I'm moving back the way I came, giving everyone a second coat.

The tin's gathering too much speed. I jump clear as it rolls off the shelf …

… and lands on one of the magpies. In fact, I do believe it's Joe. He's running in circles with the tin over his head, slamming into other birds and knocking them half out. Each and every magpie is weighed down in treacle – a slippery black blob with a beak – and they're not happy.

'Get down, Rocco, let's GO!!' someone yells.

I tear down the post at the end of the shelf – *oops – head first – not thinking straight* – and give the magpies a wide berth as I hurry across the floor after the rats, who are laden with the birds' weapons. There's just time to grab a couple of needles, and – do you know what? – I'm taking a teaspoon as well, before scrambling back up and out the basement window.

21

Foxed

Now it's straight back to the sewer, everyone choose your weapons, and hey-ho and away we go to have a little chat with a certain bunch of foxes. My trusty teaspoon served me well in the cake factory, so I'm sticking with that. In any case, it's just for show, since the foxes aren't fighters.

We line up on top of the wall at the edge of the foxes' yard. The first pink rays of dawn are in the sky, but there is no sign yet of the cunning canines. Once again Vinny is in charge.

'Come on out, you vermin!' he cries. 'We 'ave a message for ya from the Big Cheese.'

There is a sound like someone yawning loudly. It is coming from the nearest shed. And now the same sound is coming from the other one.

Maurice steps out of the shed nearest to us.

He stretches his long front legs, then he yawns again. He looks at us with a mild curiosity. At the same time, the rest of the foxes emerge from the other shed and continue with the stretching and yawning. All of us rodents are waiting on the wall, waving our kitchen utensils and shiny sharps as menacingly as possible.

'A very good morning to you too,' says Maurice. 'Please, tell us this message. If it's worth disturbing our sleep so early in the morning, then it must be extraordinary news indeed, so we're all *dying* to hear it, I'm sure.'

'Well.' Vinny clears his throat. 'We are 'ere to say that we know exactly what you riff-raff has been plottin' with them alley cats.'

Maurice lowers his brows. He looks very mean.

'And also, if you don't stop your little scheme right now, we're gonna dice you up and make six kinds of sizzlers out of ya.'

Maurice smiles. It's even scarier than the mean look.

'We'd be fascinated to see you try that,' he says, 'but unfortunately we cannot allow it. You see, none of us has any dealings whatsoever with the alley cats, and so your accusation – whatever it actually is – is plainly false. Now we foxes may be fish thieves and fakers, but we never betray, or lie to, those with whom we have made a deal.

That, my friend, is because we are *honourable*. And right now, if you won't stop threatening us, that honour of ours will see the lot of you torn to shreds without a thought for how you might be sizzled, sautéed or otherwise cooked.'

'Ha!' scoffs Vinny. 'And how are you gonna do that, then? Call the mob? Oh no, that's right – *we're* the mob!'

There are a few laughs from the rats, followed by an uneasy hush as Maurice's glare grows steelier.

'It's true that we do not use violence readily,' he says, 'because we are civilised, and prefer to let lowly creatures fight off seagulls. But we *are* foxes. We don't have to *act* deadly to *be* deadly. If you need us to prove this, we're happy to do so.'

Why is he looking at me? That'll be because *everyone* is looking at me. In fact, Vinny is staring at me with a desperate look on his face. Once again, it's down to the famous hamster to save the day.

'Fine words!' I declare. 'You say you never lie to us – but could it be that in saying so you are simply lying once more? After all, one lie leads to another, does it not? So now you threaten us, *faking* by insisting you are deadly! Because faking *is* what you do, to use your own words!'

Maurice raises an eyebrow. 'Ah yes, of course. The hamster.' His friends are sniggering. 'All right then. Tell us what it is that you think you know.'

'We don't *think* anything. I saw you with my own eyes.' This is it: the eyewitness account that they cannot deny, and it's a grand moment indeed. 'I saw you talking to that bony slip of a cat, selling your yard to her and her evil friends!'

The foxes are now laughing loudly – all except Maurice, who silences them with a wave of his paw. 'That was no alley cat you saw,' he says smugly.

'It was so! Skinny and mean-looking, and –'

'Cream-coloured, mostly, with long pointed ears and sharp face – dark in colour, those ears and that face, and the legs and tail too – slender and elegant and, ah, those striking blue eyes.' The fox pauses. 'All the features of a pure-bred Siamese.'

The rats gasp and, yes, once again they are all looking at me. There's only one thing I can say.

'What on earth is a Siamese?'

'A fancy breed of cat!' hisses Vinny. 'A pricey pet, not some good-for-nothin' stray!'

'Oh, I don't think so!' I retort. 'I am from the suburbs, a place that is *crawling* with pet cats, all fluffy and well fed! So you see, I think I know a house kitty when I see one!'

Maurice looks at me darkly. 'I'm not talking about your suburban, semi-skimmed-slurping *moggies*,' he growls. 'Our customers come to us from the west of the city – from mansions, where the humans choose their pets like they choose their sports cars.'

'What you talkin' about, *customers*?' demands Vinny. 'What you bringin' prissy pets around here for, anyway?'

But Maurice ignores him: he's too focused on me.

Stay calm, and *think*. He's lying. He must be lying. Think about everything they said, the fox and the cat.

'But you said all this would be hers, if she paid up! And who exactly are the other members of her *social circle* – the ones who're coming with her?' *I've got it.* 'And what about the *ridiculous hyperactive hamster* she promised to take care of?'

Another gasp from the rats: they'd forgotten that detail, and suddenly I'm back in the game. Maurice stands up.

'The ridiculous hamster was a birthday present for her owner's six-year-old daughter. She finds it to be an attention-seeking pest and is determined to stamp it out.' He narrows his eyes at me. 'Her social circle consists of two Persians and a Burmese who live in her neighbourhood. As for why they're coming and what they're paying for' – he nods towards the two sheds – 'you may as well come and see for yourselves.'

As he strolls off to the nearest shed, we shuffle to the gap in the wall, scramble down the broken brickwork and hurry across the yard. We peer inside the shed.

I don't know what to say. We keep looking at each other, as if checking that we're all seeing the same thing and not imagining it …

Okay, well in that case this shed appears to be the world's tiniest restaurant. There are two pink plastic tables surrounded by plump cushions, and in one corner, a stack of little china plates and bowls, all matching.

'What's all this then?' asks Vinny. 'Some kinda *boutique bistro*?'

Maurice smiles. 'We like to think so. You see, while you rats steal scraps with which to stuff your own faces, *we* are running a successful restaurant. A seafood restaurant, to be precise. Those cats do like a good piece of fish.'

'We didn't know you was runnin' a business!' says Vinny. 'Why didn't you tell us?'

'You never asked.'

'What do the cats pay you with?' I ask, although I don't even care about the answer.

The fox shrugs. 'Go on over to the other shed and take a look.'

We drift across the yard and look inside. All right. So the foxes are living in a palace of plush cat beds and soft fleecy blankets. I have seen enough. I want to go back to the sewer and stick my head in some stinking water.

But Vinny's not finished yet.

'Very impressive, Maurice,' he's saying, but in a dangerous tone of voice. 'You seem to be makin' a very *comfortable* profit, bringin' cats into our backyard. You did say *cats*, didn't you, Maurice? As in felines? Kitties? Adorable, purrin', scratchin', rodent-killin' balls of fluff?'

Maurice's smile broadens. 'The very same.'

There is an uneasy murmur among the rats.

'Well what do we think of that?' asks Vinny. 'Do we let these mutts play their little game of *restaurants* with our hated foes? Alley cats or pampered Persians, it's all the same! I say we dice 'em up anyways!'

The uneasy murmur turns into a riot of angry yelling. Everyone is waving their weapons, and they're beginning to surround Maurice. But there's a menacing light in the fox's eye.

'Have our guests ever troubled you?' he snaps. 'Of course not! They're overfed and upper crust and they've no interest whatsoever in chasing sewer rats!'

'They don't mind murdering hamsters,' I hear myself mutter.

'We're the mob around here,' Vinny continues, 'the ultimate business critters. That means we get to decide what goes on and who goes *down* in this neighbourhood!'

Maurice takes a step towards Vinny, his fur

bristling, gums pulled back in a snarl that reveals long white teeth. 'You're even more foolish than you looked when you were standing on the wall with a cheese grater! *You need us*, remember? We're the only thing keeping those alley cats away from your smelly rotten sewer pipes! And besides, do you *really* doubt that we could bite your rodent heads off at any moment – if we had to?'

The other foxes have formed a circle around us. Now you know how I pride myself on my awesome displays of fighting skills, but there's more than one way to save the day.

'YES, OF COURSE! AND NO, OF COURSE NOT! THANK YOU SO MUCH FOR YOUR TIME!!'

And with that we're off, Vinny included, tearing past the foxes and through the gap in the wall …

We're all running as fast as we can, of course, but my legs are a little shorter than the rats'. I glance over my shoulder: the foxes are not following us. I drop back, let the others race on ahead. To be honest, I'm not really feeling my best right now, and I'm in no hurry to return to the sewer …

I don't mind telling you that I've just collapsed in a heap twenty feet from our front door, the drainpipe under the bridge.

'Rocco!'

Was that Nev? It takes all my energy just to look up. But yes, it is Nev, running along the bank towards me. He looks panicky.

'It wasn't an owl!' he says, in a kind of shouted whisper. 'In the park! *It wasn't an owl!*'

'What are you talking about?'

'Just now, I … was throwing away our sweetie packet …' Nev is even more out of breath than I am. 'And I noticed … some little feathers … stuck in the sugar …'

'And?'

'They're not owl feathers! *They're pigeon feathers!*'

As a rule, pigeons don't go out and about at night. Except, perhaps, one.

'Francis Pigeoni,' I murmur.

'Exactly. And he's already had plenty of time to tell the alley cats about our trip to see Dwayne. Meaning they now know we have a spy – and they know where to find him.'

'Then Dwayne's in danger. And he's—'

'Unable to tell any lies. Whatever they ask, he's going to tell them the whole truth.' Nev is already scrambling up the bank. 'We have to get to the park – right now!'

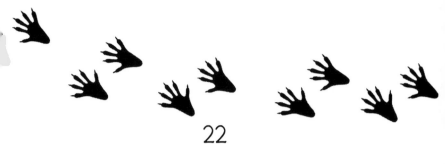

22

Saving Dwayne

Thankfully, it's still too early for most humans to be up and about. This means that we have just managed to run the whole way to the park without having to scrabble through hedges. Now that we've reached the gates, we have to tread carefully. My head is spinning, and my heart is thumping in my ears.

'I hope we're in time,' I whisper, and I mean it. After this morning's episode with the foxes, I'm not in great shape for battling our feline foes.

Nev is scanning the open ground between us and Dwayne's molehills. 'There's no sign of anyone,' he says. 'Let's make a run for it!'

We scurry across the grass … but before we even reach the nearest molehill, it's plain to see that something is very wrong. Dwayne's muddy mound has been flattened, torn down, broken into clumps of earth tossed far and wide.

It has been *dug into*.

We hurry from one molehill to the next – all have been smashed to bits in the same way.

'Dwayne!' calls Nev. 'Dwayne, are you there? It's Nev and Rocco!'

We're running around on the scattered soil. It's like a churned-up battlefield.

'Maybe he got out in time,' I say hopefully. 'He's very clever, with those tunnels of his. Perhaps he escaped.'

'But where did he go?' Nev seems to whisper that question to the world in general.

I point to the nearest trees. 'We could start over there.'

It's the best guess we have, so we make for the trees. You might expect we'd feel safer under there, but this is not the case. To creatures our size, a small group of trees may as well be a vast forest, with the danger of enemies lurking behind every trunk.

Together we pick our way between the roots. This could take a while, if no one risks a whisper, so here goes:

'*Dwayne!*'

We listen: nothing. I scramble over twigs, dodge between conkers; I'm moving as fast as I can now, and I know Nev is right behind me.

We stop. We sniff the air. There's a faint rustling sound, somewhere off to the right. I creep towards it, Nev at my side. If I'm honest, I'm expecting a great big ugly cat to come leaping out of nowhere and swallow us whole. But I have to pull myself together. I won't abandon Dwayne to a horrible fate.

'We're getting close,' Nev whispers.

We crawl behind a tree root and peer over the top. Straight ahead, there is a little pile of leaves. It is trembling.

'Dwayne?' says Nev.

The pile stops trembling. Very slowly, a pink nose emerges. 'Nev?'

We hurry over, pull Dwayne from under the leaves and dust the dirt from him.

'That wasn't such a great hiding place,' I tell him. 'The best hiding places don't usually shake so much.'

'Thank heavens we found you first,' adds Nev. 'Francis saw us, the night we visited you. We've seen what those cats did to the molehills.'

'Well ... the thing is,' says Dwayne. We stop dusting his fur. 'Actually, you didn't find me first ... I mean ... I ...' He bursts into tears. 'They knew our signal! They tossed the little stone into the side of the molehill, and out I popped! Right into their paws!' I hand him a leaf and he blows his nose. 'I'm sorry!'

Nev sags, burying his face in his hands.

'What did they do to you?' I ask, more than a little afraid of the answer.

'Oh, well they … pinned me down with their claws, and … asked me some … some questions.'

'What questions?'

'Oh, you know, um … questions about the gang. About … the whereabouts of the gang's lair.'

Nev's wide eyes are peering between his fingers. I can hardly bear to ask Dwayne the obvious question … but here it comes:

'What did you tell them?'

'*Everything!*' Dwayne is now sobbing uncontrollably. 'Where the – entrances are to the – rats' den! And – I told them – the rats might just have – fallen out with the foxes! Who aren't – vicious and – aren't even interested in fighting!'

'All right, let's look at this calmly,' says Nev, although his voice is trembling. 'It's not safe for you to stay in the park. The cats might come back, or else the rats, once they figure out that you …'

'I think what Nev is trying to say,' I add helpfully, 'is that you should come back to the docklands with us. There you can hide out somewhere and stay safe from some very angry rats, while we plan how to destroy the alley cats, who will, of course, be launching their attack on our sewer very soon.'

No one seems particularly happy about that analysis, but they're not disagreeing with it either, so without further ado we're heading home. The fishmonger's van should be delivering to the big houses opposite the park right about now, with Salty's Seafood Bistro its next stop. That means we can hitch a lift back to the docks without fear of being spotted.

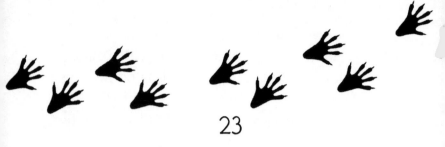

23

It's Not Lying, It's Self-preservation

The Jolly Yachtsman Hotel seems to be collecting beer kegs by its back door. One of these kegs is now occupied by a very anxious Dwayne.

Of course, this is strictly between Nev, and me, and you. No one else must know about it – not even Nev's family. They'll be safer that way – if they know nothing, the rats can't punish them for being involved – and they'll also be unable to accidentally spill the beans.

Nev and I are hurrying to the chamber right now. I suppose it's safe to say that I am not very popular at the moment. After all, our scuffle with the magpies was not, it turns out, necessary; it was all for the sake of gathering weapons for an alley cat invasion that was never going to happen. Because the foxes were not in fact plotting to sell their territory to the alley cats after all. Which brings us to the other, near-fatal brush with the foxes. And yes, Nev and I are about to break the news that now the alley cats *really are coming after all* – all because Francis Pigeoni spotted Nev and me visiting Dwayne … a visit that only happened because I thought the alley cats were coming, when they weren't …

Okay, so when you think about it like that you *could* say all of this is my fault. But Nev and I have been thinking fast. Which is lucky, because here we are, entering the chamber.

Everyone is here. Everyone looks mad. Must START TALKING before someone remembers they want to kill me.

'The alley cats! The alley cats are coming! No – this time they *really are*! Honest!'

It's all about speaking confidently.

'Can it, hamster, it's gettin' old! If you're tryin' to buy yourself some time before we gobble up your gizzard, you're gonna have to do better than that!'

I don't even know who said that, but I'm very keen to do as they suggest. Thankfully, Nev and I have it all worked out. Dwayne's part in all this must not be mentioned – so a tiny lie must be told.

'Francis told us! He was drinking out of a

puddle, and we sprang on him! We nailed his feathery behind to the wall and demanded that he give us some news!' I just this moment made that last bit up. I think it was rather good.

'That's exactly what happened,' drones Nev. I feel he could have said that a little more as if he meant it.

'AND WHY IS IT THE ALLEY CATS DECIDE TO PAY US A VISIT *RIGHT NOW*?' asks the Big Cheese. 'DID THE PIGEON SPY THE LOT OF YA OVER AT THE FOXES', ALL WEAPONS AND THREATS AND KICKIN' UP A FUSS ABOUT *CATS*?'

'Maybe,' yells someone, 'they thought that since we've fallen out big time with our only allies, this might be a good time to move in, strike a deal with them foxes and separate us from our well-fed guts!'

'Just like you said was gonna happen! Except it *wasn't* gonna happen! And now it really *is* gonna happen!'

'Yeah!'

'IT'S ALL YOUR FAULT!'

I know it looks like a bad situation, but in fact this is one mess I can talk my way out of.

'Actually, friends, according to the pigeon those cats are coming right now, as quick as their grubby paws can carry them, because they've heard all about my awesome greatness! Especially how I *sweetened up* those magpies! They feel threatened – so they thought they'd spring a surprise attack! But they've failed already, haven't they? Thanks, I believe, to me and my partner in crime Nev!'

Most of the rats have begun chattering, but some – including Vinny – are glaring at me with a new kind of malice. Nev looks at me uncertainly.

'SO YOU'RE SAYIN' ALL OF THIS IS A GOOD THING?'

'Yes!' I've got it. I've nailed it. 'Don't you see? We can meet them head-on! Take *them* by surprise! This is our chance to destroy those alley cats once and for all!'

Frenzied excitement all around. Even Vinny seems to be giving this some thought. Only Nev is shaking his head frantically.

'ALL RIGHT! THE 'AMSTER HAS A POINT. AS USUAL. SO STOP STANDIN' AROUND AND GET OUT THERE! WITH UTENSILS!'

24

Cat-astrophe

'I'm going,' says Tina. 'I'm going, I'm going, I'm *so* going.'

Here's the deal: while the rest of us are busy taking down the cats, the mice will spread out and search the docklands for any scouts – cats who're already in the neighbourhood, trying to gather info on us before the others arrive.

Or, to be more precise, the *grown-up* mice will search the docklands.

'You're not going anywhere, Tina,' says her mum. 'You and Pip are to stay right here.'

Nev is lying in a heap on the floor. This is because, to be even *more* precise, all the grown-up mice except Nev will be searching the docklands. After all, Nev has proved himself as a gangster by taking part in the assault on Francis (the one that didn't technically happen), and the rats have insisted that he must join the fight.

'*Nev's* going!' cries Tina. 'Nev's *fighting*! If Nev can fight, why can't I?'

'Because,' says Nev, 'I am going to be chewed up and spat out by a mangy cat, and someone has to stay alive to keep the family going. Karate kicks are not going to be any use, Tina. Besides, the rats don't want to be laughed at, which is exactly what'll happen if they show up with a little kid mouse wearing a shoelace on her head.'

'It's a bandana!'

'You should have more confidence in yourself, Nev,' I try. He's giving me a weary look. 'After all, you never know what you're capable of, until you try. Who knows what you can do, if you're determined enough? Those cats are coming – that much is certain – and we'll never survive if we give up hope already.'

Everyone is looking at me in surprise. I think they understand my meaning, and in their hearts I think they feel the same way.

Now Nev is getting to his feet. He's coming over … and he's giving my shoulder a squeeze.

'Come on, Rocco,' he says. 'Let's get going.'

Everyone agrees that as the cats believe they have the element of surprise, they will not bother to sneak into the docklands through the backstreets but will come as quick as they can, by the most direct route. Therefore, we are lined up in the yard behind the Scuttled Frigate pub, waiting for them.

Of course, we're all armed to the teeth with top-quality kitchenware (you should check out my pastry fork – even more dangerous than the teaspoon) and the magpies' shiniest bits and bobs. All except Nev, who has strapped a tub of toothpicks to his back. We've been here an hour already, but there's still no sign of the alley cats.

The rats are growing restless.

'Either the 'amster's 'aving us on,' says Vinny, 'or old Francis made the whole thing up. Because if them cats was on their way like he said, they'd have got 'ere ages ago. They're only comin' from the alley beside the twenty-four-hour minimart.'

'And we didn't see 'em on the way,' says another rat, 'so they can't have come by already.'

'Unless they went some other way,' suggests a third.

'But they wouldn't, so we said!' the second rat protests. 'Element of surprise and all that, we said, remember?'

'Of course,' says Vinny, rubbing his chin thoughtfully, 'it's always possible them cats *know* their element of surprise is busted. Supposin' they saw Pigeoni spyin' on 'em, gettin' an earful of their evil plans, then flyin' off towards the docks.

Then they'd know we *know*, wouldn't they, and they'd go by some roundabout route, laughin' just to think of us sittin' 'ere like fools while they move in on our territory.'

There is a long and uncomfortable silence.

'So what do we do, Vinny?'

'We waits 'ere a little bit longer. If they 'ave gone some other way we're too late to stop 'em, and the mice'll have spied 'em out for us when we gets back. But all of that is a big *what if*. I'll bet all of them are right nearby, cookin' up some plan that we'll crush in no time. Speakin' of which, who said you could 'ave the potato masher, Spike?'

As the rats begin squabbling over who should have what weapon, Nev pulls me to one side.

'Rocco,' he whispers, 'what if they *have* gone another way?'

'Well,' I tell him, 'so long as they believe in their element of surprise—'

'But we *invented* that element of surprise! Just like we *invented* the idea that they're attacking us because they're frightened of some hamster!'

That smarts a little, until I remember that it's absolutely true.

'They're attacking because …' – Nev is having a moment of realisation, and I can tell he's not enjoying it one bit – 'because they found out we have a spy, and they found out *from* our spy exactly where we live, which is information they could never get close enough to find out for themselves, thanks to the foxes … The foxes, who they've now heard are not quite as dangerous as they seem. Now for all they know we've already found out from Dwayne that he told them everything.'

'You mean … they know they might *not* have the element of surprise.'

'Exactly.'

'In which case … they also know this might just be the worst route they could possibly choose.'

'They do indeed.'

This is terrible. While we've been standing in this dusty yard, those foul cats have no doubt been zigzagging their way through the narrowest, grubbiest backstreets between here and the docks. How did I fail to realise what a sticky mess we're in? The answer hits me like a rock. I have believed my own lies – the ones about threatening Francis, about being feared by the cats; the ones that brought us to this yard. I've been too caught up in boastful bluffing, and have completely lost track of the truth.

'Their mucky paws could be tramping over our fine cobbled streets already,' I whisper.

'And my family's out on those streets.'

We look steadily at each other. I'll say what we're both thinking:

'We have to get back, right now.'

'Yes we do.'

The rats are still fighting over the weaponry. Apparently, everyone wants that potato masher.

'The tricky part is persuading all of *them* that we should go back now,' says Nev.

I nod thoughtfully. Yet no matter how hard I think, I have absolutely no idea what to say or do. Alarmingly, it seems that Nev doesn't either.

Our efforts at figuring this out are interrupted by something white and gooey, splatting on to the ground barely an inch from where Nev is standing.

It is bird mess.

I am about to say, 'That was close,' but Nev's gaze is already fixed on the source, high above us. I look up, craning my neck. Perched on a lamp post right over our heads is none other than Francis Pigeoni. If it's possible for someone with tiny beads for eyes and a beak in place of a mouth, I'd say Francis looks embarrassed.

Nev and I look at each other. Our genius minds are thinking alike.

'Hey there Francis!' I yell.

The rats stop squabbling. Three dozen heads turn to the lamp post. That's seventy-two yellow eyeballs, and there's burning suspicion in every one.

'It's the pigeon!' someone shouts. 'Who may or may not have been seen by the cats!'

'And ruined everythin' – possibly!'

'Let's kill 'im! Just in case!'

There are snarls of agreement, and lots of stainless steel being waved in the air. Those at the front start scuttling towards the lamp post.

'WAIT!!' screams Nev. 'He's occasionally useful, remember? He might have information for us.'

'The mouse is right,' growls Vinny. 'He already told us the cats is comin'. If that ain't a lie.'

Everyone backs away from the lamp post, muttering their disappointment. For a moment there I was worried that Francis might point out that he *didn't* tell us the cats are coming – but he seems happy to take the credit.

'Although,' adds Vinny suddenly, 'I don't know how *useful* he really is – after all, you two almost had to beat him up to get that information on the cats ...'

The rats nod and chatter. Francis is staring at Nev and me.

I sense Nev's panic.

It's contagious.

'Eh, well,' I try, 'we only, I mean, we didn't really, you know, that's not how it, I mean ... I might have ... *exaggerated* a bit.'

Vinny raises an eyebrow. As does Francis. I try shrugging to say I'm sorry, but my heart is hammering in my chest.

'Right, whatever,' shouts Vinny. 'Why don't

you get down here right now, Pigeoni, and tell us everythin' you've got on them alley cats. And it better be good!'

By clamping my lips tight shut, I manage not to let out a huge gasp of relief. My fibbing back in the sewer didn't just make *me* sound extra fantastically superb – it made *Francis* sound bad and nearly got him wiped out. Yet the pigeon flutters calmly to the ground, untroubled by the fact that nearly everyone present wants to kill him for some misguided reason. In fact, for a moment he simply stands, very upright, as though enjoying the power that his knowledge gives him.

And now … now he is placing his wings behind his head, running on the spot … pointing to the right …

'What's he *doing*?' I hiss in Nev's ear.

'Telling us everything he's got,' whispers Nev, as if it's obvious. 'Francis doesn't talk. He mimes.'

He's hopping up and down with the tips of his wings sticking up behind his head – like pointed ears. All at once, the rats start to guess.

'Cat …'

'Cats running …'

He jabs the air with both wings, pointing …

'To the docks!' I cry. He nods at me. I'm quite enjoying this now.

'But we know that already!' someone yells. 'That's why we're standing 'ere!'

Francis shakes his head. He raises the tips of his wings behind his head again.

'*CATS!!*'

Next he lies on the ground, one leg over the other, wings crossed behind his head.

'Sunbathing!'

'Relaxing!'

Francis hops to his feet. With his feathery fingers politely splayed, he saws the air with an imaginary something-or-other held in his right wing … stabs it with something in his left … lifts it to his beak, which is click-click-clicking as he pretends to eat …

'Fine dining,' announces Vinny.

'Oh no,' whispers Nev, 'the cats are eating food from the restaurants. They're already at the docks.'

Francis turns to Nev and gives him two thumbs up (or two feathers, at least).

'WHAT?!' hollers Vinny. 'You mean those pointy-eared vermin are thieving our haute cuisine?!' He snatches up the potato masher. '*BACK TO THE DOCKS! NOW!!*'

The rats have headed straight for the chamber to report back to the Big Cheese – but not so Nev and I. We met neither cat nor mouse as we tore through the streets on our way back to the sewer, so the first thing to do is to find Pip and Tina and warn them of the danger.

We tumble into the mouse house and flop down on the floor, breathless. There's no one here.

Actually, I can hear a muffled banging. And a muffled call of 'Help.' Nev's heard it too, and we're back on our feet, looking frantically around the room.

In a shadowy corner, a tall jar is rocking back and forth. We hurry over. Inside is a very hot-and-bothered Pip, standing with his hands and face pressed to the glass. 'Let me out,' he says.

'Hold on!' says Nev.

We hop up the staircase of matchboxes stacked behind the jar, unscrew the lid, and push. The jar topples on to its side with a *clink*, and Pip rolls out on to the floor.

'Are you all right?' I ask as we help him to his feet. 'What happened?'

'You mean … *who* happened,' he pants.

Nev looks at him sideways. 'Where's Tina?' he asks.

'How should I know?' grumbles Pip. 'She ran off as soon as she had me stuck in that jar.'

'Tina did that to you?' I can't help feeling impressed.

'She told me that my efforts to stop her going outside proved I am an honourable mouse, but it's her destiny to save our streets from invasion. And then she left.'

'When?' says Nev.

'At least an hour ago, I think. Although time does tend to drag, when you're *in a jar*.'

Now we're rushing through the sewer while trying to tell Pip all that has happened. There's daylight ahead, but it's casting the long shadow of a mystery creature, standing right in our doorway. We slow down, creeping forward and squinting into the bright light. Finally, I can make out not one, but three figures – very small ones, scurrying down the pipe towards us.

It's Nev's parents and Uncle Alfie.

'You're all right!' shouts Nev's mum, grabbing Nev and me in a hug.

'What happened?' asks his dad. 'We saw that idiot Vinny leaping down a drain waving a potato masher.'

'The cats are already here,' blurts Nev. 'You didn't see them?'

'No,' says Uncle Alfie. 'We looked everywhere, except the restaurants.'

'Tina's out there too,' says Pip. Now Nev's mum looks like she's about to faint, so we hurry up the pipe and out into the sunshine.

We make for the bridge, busy with cars and people. Knowing Tina, she'll be weaving between their wheels and under their feet without a thought for anything other than kung fu kicking those cats.

We run up the embankment ... round the

end of the iron railings that run the length of the bridge —

Oomph.

Straight into something small and wide-eyed. The mice land in a pile on top of me.

So we've found Tina, then.

I may be lying beneath a heap of furry bodies, but something tells me that Tina is already back on her feet.

'Come on! Hurry!'

Everyone scrambles off me, and before I can even get up, Tina has rolled me back on to the embankment and under the shadow of the bridge.

She hardly needs to explain that she has stumbled upon the alley cats.

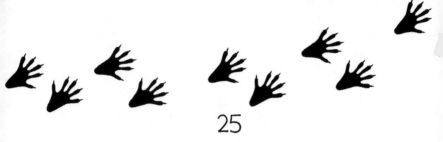

Well They Should Have Signed a Contract

Tina is standing on an upturned yogurt pot. Everyone in the chamber is listening to her with open mouths.

'Two of them, right? Round the back of Chef Claude's. A massive, bushy tabby and a big ginger tom with a chewed-up ear. And Chef Claude's there too. They're rubbin' against him, and he's giving it some French-talk, like, "'Ello, leettle kittees, 'ow are you today, you would like some feesh, no?" And then he goes back into the kitchen—'

Tina pauses to bounce high on her yogurt pot, kicking and punching the air.

'—and then, out he comes again, with fish! And he gives it to those scruffy cats!'

There is a gasp of horror from the crowd.

'And then he tickles them under their big ugly chins, and he says, "Ah, nice kittees! Zer is plenty more of zat lovely feesh for you! You can stay 'ere, and soon you will get reed of all zose dirty rats, oui?"'

Cries of outrage all around.

'So then I run round the front, and there are two more! A thin, smoky grey one, and a black one with one eye and four white socks. Sitting prim as you like on Claude's front doorstep.'

Much tut-tutting and shaking of heads.

'That's when I knew I had to come get backup!' Tina leaps from the yogurt pot and makes for the exit. 'Let's go get 'em, while they're still at Claude's!'

Suddenly, the rats' anger turns into a lot of muttering and shuffling of feet.

'HANG ON A SECOND.' The Big Cheese, at last. 'THE MOUSE IS RIGHT. WE 'AVE TO TAKE THEM CATS DOWN, AND DO IT FAST. BUT 'ERE'S THE THING: YOU LOT GO OUT THERE RIGHT NOW, AND YOU MIGHT JUST GET EATEN UP FASTER THAN THEM FISH. SO 'ERE'S WHAT I SAY: GO GET THE FOXES. TELL 'EM TO STRUT THEIR STUFF, ALL VICIOUS LIKE.'

'But they won't help! Last time we paid 'em a visit we attacked 'em!' protests Vinny.

'NO YOU DIDN'T. YOU ONLY THREATENED TO ATTACK 'EM.'

'And,' I chip in, 'we politely took it back once they explained what was really going on. The thing is, they can't risk our gang getting wiped out, because they still want us around to see off the gulls every day. And besides, I'm sure an alley cat invasion won't go down well with their customers. So actually, I think they'll be glad to help, and they won't just *act* vicious, either.'

''COURSE NOT. THEM CATS 'AVE GOT TOO BIG FOR THEIR BOOTS IF THEY WANNA PLAY ROUGH WITH THAT LOT. NOW GET OUT THERE AND CUT THEM DOWN TO SIZE. WITH HELP.'

Every one of us is staring in disbelief at the foxes, who are standing in the middle of their yard beside a pull-along wagon loaded with luxury cat beds. They were already gathered there when we came pouring through the gap in the wall.

And the reason they were already gathered there is this: they are leaving. That's right. Upping sticks. Shipping out. They have packed their plush pillows, along with their tables and crockery, and are ready to go.

'So sorry we can't help,' says Maurice, not at all as if he means it, 'but you see we're right in the middle of moving to the suburbs.'

'But … *why*?' splutters Vinny.

'Oh, that's simple. We wish to expand our

successful business. I mean, fine dining is all well and good, but we thought, what the heck – let's go for the mass market. And I believe that when you last paid us a visit, your hamster mentioned that the suburbs have a large population of pet cats. So I suppose we should thank him for giving us the idea.'

I sneak back over the wall and dash up the lane before anyone can quite take in what the fox just said.

26

Murder by Meatballs

The atmosphere within the sewer is extremely tense. Everyone is laying low, but no one is laying lower than me.

It's all my fault the cats are here.

It's all my fault the foxes aren't.

Three days have passed since Maurice and company moved to the suburbs. Within that time I have experienced many new emotions, and I haven't enjoyed a single one of them. First came *guilt*, then a *total loss of confidence* and some serious *despair*. Today's addition to the list is *utter hopelessness*. Of course, everyone around me is sharing in it, except for Tina. She alone is asking why we don't just storm the streets and beat up the cats with rolling pins, or even our bare little hands.

This morning she asked me that question for the fourteenth time. The conversation went something like this:

'But Rocco, why don't *you* want to go bust up those cats, just like we used to talk about?'

'Because they're big and fierce, and they'll eat us.'

I may have broken her heart, but that's better than watching her get eaten by a flea-bitten feline. There's nothing shameful in knowing when you're beaten. In fact, knowing when you're beaten allows you to avoid *total* disaster. It allows you to stay *alive*.

I can hear Nev hurrying through the pipe. He sticks his head inside the mouse house.

'The rats are getting seriously grumpy with hunger,' he says. 'We better go quick, before they remember that we're protein.'

Ah yes, I haven't told you yet, have I? Now that the cats have moved in and the foxes have moved out, the mice (and that includes me) have food-collecting duty all to ourselves. The rats are doing none of the restaurant raids, supposedly because they are larger and more easily spotted by the cats. But you know the real reason as well as I do: they're too scared to go outside. So, to avoid becoming lunch ourselves, we're doing our best to fill up their stomachs three times daily. Trouble is, even with my cheek pouches full to bursting, we simply can't carry enough and everyone is permanently hungry – and increasingly angry about it.

So without further ado, we're all running up the pipe towards the exit. But someone is blocking our path up ahead. I immediately recognise the fussiest eater in the sewer. He claims he's *gluten free*. I don't know what that means, but I do know that he refuses to eat almost everything we collect.

'Hello there Benny,' says Nev's dad, nervously. 'Any special requests today? We'll do our best, as always.'

'I'll save you the trouble,' says Benny. 'See, you idiot mice can't seem to get to grips with the simplest of dietary needs, so this time I'm comin' with you.'

What a treat.

'Oh, well … all right then,' says Nev's dad. 'Which restaurant is it to be?'

'The very best,' declares Benny. 'Let's see what Claude's got on the specials board.'

'Just you make sure your stupid great furry hugeness doesn't get us noticed by those cats!' says Tina, as Nev places a hand across her mouth.

So that's settled then: off we go, into the danger zone with Benny. Let's all hope the signs are out for Gluten Day à la Claude.

***

Thankfully, at this time of day the chef himself is away at the market. In fact, only one of his cooks is in the kitchen, and right now he is snoozing in a chair with a magazine draped over his face. This seems unwise, as something is sizzling furiously in the frying pan, but it suits us just fine.

My cheeks are already loaded with cherries. Nev and Tina are positioned at either end of a huge baguette, with Cousin Pip holding it up in the middle. As the baguette hurries across the floor, Nev's parents and Uncle Alfie are carefully sliding wedges of cheese off a huge wooden board.

I look around for something I can carry. And what do I see but Benny, standing on the work surface next to the cooker, fanning smoke from the frying pan towards himself and sniffing dreamily.

'*Benny!*' I hiss. 'What are you doing up there?'

'What does it look like?' he sneers. 'I'm 'elping myself to the good stuff while you lot scrabble about the floor with bread and cheese.'

'But we don't take cooked things, not these days. We can't carry enough for everyone and it causes fights.'

'Trust me,' says Benny, 'when the others get a whiff of what you mice have left behind, you'll be comin' back 'ere in relays till we've *all* had our fill.'

He's doing an evil laugh, but I've already turned away. There's a pile of pastries on the table, so I climb up a string of onions hanging over the edge, and sling a croissant on to my back.

The cook snorts loudly. We all freeze. He's still sound asleep, but all the same, it's time to go.

'Where's Benny?' asks Nev's mum.

We look around. The rat has already gone.

'I'm afraid he's made off with whatever's cooking in that frying pan,' I tell them.

'I knew it,' sighs Nev's dad. 'Ah well, it can't be helped.'

We're all peering out of the door. The coast seems to be clear, so we make a dash for it.

How I'd love to tell you that we're safely back in the chamber, with the rats happily filling their faces. But instead we're on the bank under the bridge, along with Benny … and a few other interested individuals.

It's the seagulls. With the foxes and their seafood gone, they're clearly looking for a whole new food fight. And right now they're looking straight at us. We're facing each other in two lines: eight of us, five of them, but all the same I don't like those odds. The gulls are standing between us and our front door.

'Clear off!' yells Benny. 'I'll wring yer scrawny necks before I'll give up a crumb!'

Indeed, it's Benny's frazzled mixture of meat and herbs that has captured the gulls' attention.

Apparently it is known as a *meatball*, and Benny has pinched three of them. The gulls don't budge, although the one in the middle lowers his head, stretching a menacing beak towards Benny.

Nev gives me a nudge. 'Something's not right,' he whispers. 'Claude never has meatballs on his menu.'

'He doesn't?'

'Of course not! They're Italian, not French.'

'Oh. Well, in that case …' I'm hoping we can now resolve the situation swiftly, because this croissant is starting to feel heavy. 'Actually,' I announce, 'there could be something funny about those meatballs.'

Benny glares at me. 'Oh yeah? And why is that?'

'Because they're Italian and Claude only cooks French. I don't think he'd be giving those to his customers.'

Benny laughs loudly. 'Of course!' he jeers. 'He made them *specially for us*!'

Out the corner of my eye, I am aware of that middle seagull waddling down the bank, straight towards Benny. But the rat is too busy mocking me to notice.

'Right on cue, the 'amster blows in like so much hot air! Well, my friend, if you say don't eat the meatball, then 'ere's to the delicious meatball!'

Benny opens his mouth wide to take a bite, just as the seagull opens his beak.

I drop my croissant.

Dive towards Benny.

Bowl him out of the way as the gull's beak snaps shut on thin air.

'Aaaarrggh!' cries Benny. 'You idiot—!'

'Aaaarrggh!' That's me this time, I'm afraid, because the gull is coming in for another go – but Nev, Tina and Pip knock him out of the picture with their baguette battering ram.

The other gulls are shrieking, beating their wings and running at us.

'Quick!' yells Nev's dad. 'Use what you've brought, then make for the door!'

He and Nev's mum and Uncle Alfie are flinging cheese at the birds' heads, while the baguette, with Tina at the leading end, is storming back and forth jabbing each of the gulls in turn. As for me, I'm spitting cherries like rounds of machine gun fire.

But Benny is less willing to participate.

'YOU IDIOT HAMSTER!' he's yelling in my ear, over the gulls' screeches and Tina's war cries. 'YOU MADE ME DROP THAT MEATBALL! AND WHERE D'YOU THINK IT IS NOW?!'

I pause in my cherry-spitting. 'I've no idea!'

Benny points at the dark river behind us. 'AT THE BOTTOM OF *THAT* LOT, THAT'S WHERE!'

'Don't worry!' I tell him. 'You've got two more! Just throw those, they're good and heavy!'

'HAVE YOU LOST YER TINY MIND?! I AIN'T THROWIN' THEM, I'M *EATIN'* THEM!'

'Not if he eats them first!' shouts Nev.

We turn quickly. The gulls' leader is holding one of Benny's treasured meatballs in his beak. The other gulls are squawking excitedly, trying to get the third one – but he's got it clamped under his big webbed foot.

Nev's parents and Uncle Alfie have run out of cheese; I think the gulls have eaten it all. Only the baguette has survived – with many chunks torn off – to make a final, desperate lunge across the grassy bank.

Too late.

'NOOOOO!!'

As Benny dives towards him, the seagull swallows down the last of the blackened meat, and clicks his beak in satisfaction. Benny freezes. His eyes are bulging and his jaw is twitching, as though he's about to go into some kind of fit. His crazy stare drops towards the last remaining meatball, which the gull keeps rolling in little circles under the tip of his toe, apparently just to upset Benny.

The gull has an altogether smug look about him.

Well, actually, he *did* have a smug look, but now it's gone. Suddenly, I'd say he looks a bit queasy. His eyeballs are rolling around. His tongue is hanging out of his beak. Now he's making a kind of strangled clucking sound. He wraps both wings around his throat, wheezing, staggering first to the left, then to the right.

The meatball rolls free, but no one's touching it.

The seagull has gone rigid. His left foot lifts off the ground ... he's sort of – twirling on his right.

Nobody moves. The seagull falls over backwards, stiffly. His feet are in the air.

The other gulls stare at him blankly, or perhaps their faces just can't do anything else. At last one of them gives a single squawk.

The mice and Benny and I shuffle closer.

'Is he – dead?' asks Benny.

'I should think that's more than obvious,' I can't help saying.

One by one we back off, heading for the pipe. Benny has a last, longing look at that third meatball before scurrying after.

As we move inside, I look over my shoulder at the seagulls, still standing next to their fallen comrade. I have to admit, I feel rather sorry for them.

'BLIMEY.'

Everyone waits, but it seems that this is all the Big Cheese has to say about one of the seagulls being killed by Chef Claude's meatball.

'They're poisoned,' says Nev. 'And I don't mean they've gone bad, I mean Claude put poison in them.'

'But he wouldn't be giving poisoned meatballs to his customers!' someone points out.

'Then the 'amster was right!' wails Benny. 'That good-for-nothin' cook left 'em out for us to steal!'

'Does anyone smell something?' asks a rat at the back of the crowd. Everyone lifts their snouts and sniffs hard. There is a warm, herby aroma mixed with the stale air of the sewer. As we keep sniffing, it's getting stronger.

'Sage, and ...'

'Thyme. Definitely thyme.'

'And beef ... lots of juicy, pan-fried —'

'Meatballs!' yells Vinny. 'At the front door!'

Everyone is running to and fro in utter confusion.

'GO, GO, GO!' shouts the Big Cheese.

Now the rats are making for the doorway under the bridge. The mice and I gather close and run behind them.

At the end of the pipe, we push our way through the crowd, and there it is: a big pile of meatballs. The rats stare at them in horror, and fear, and fury – and their mouths are watering. One or two begin drifting towards the pile as though under a spell, and have to be pulled back.

After all, two webbed feet are still sticking up in the air just a little way down the bank.

'Split up!' Vinny shouts. 'Search the bank! I wanna know *everything* these villains are up to!'

The rats pour left and right along the embankment; some dive into the water and swim for the other side. As I shoot towards the cobbled lane beside the Jolly Yachtsman, along with the mice and a handful of rats, we can already see the full extent of the trouble.

For all along the water's edge are cooks from Chef Claude's kitchen, in their white jackets and checked trousers, sprinkling treacherous treats by every hole and crevice leading into our sewer. And leading them, guiding them from one *secret* doorway to the next, are none other than the alley cats, skipping and meowing.

And look – there's Claude with his tabby and ginger friends, just like Tina described them. They're dancing round his ankles as he merrily deposits generous helpings of death. Suddenly it all makes sense: Claude wasn't at the market while we were raiding his kitchen – he and his team were already out here on their evil mission, except for the one cook left behind, who was supposed to be looking after the next batch of meatballs.

Actually, Claude's big clogs are stomping this way, so we retreat into the lane. No one can speak.

Even Tina looks worried. Claude thunders past the end of the lane, and keeps going.

Now here comes Vinny. 'Regroup!' he cries as he streaks past.

Everyone gathers behind the Jolly Yachtsman's wheelie bins. Vinny returns with the last of the rats. He has a mad glimmer in his eyes.

'Okay,' he pants. 'So ... what do we know ... We know Claude's tryin' to poison us, and those filthy cats is 'elping him because they know where we live.' Vinny is wheezing like crazy, and everyone's leaning back as though afraid he might explode. 'DID YOU HEAR WHAT I SAID?!! THEY KNOW WHERE WE LIVE! *HOW* DO THEY KNOW WHERE WE LIVE?!!'

'Dunno, boss,' says one rat. 'No one knows where our doors are 'cept for us.'

'*Well* ...' says another, 'there is *one* other critter who knows ...'

Oh no. Oh heck. I can feel a cold sweat coming on. Nev is shaking. Vinny is boiling over, gurgling in his throat, and vibrating.

'DWAAAYYYYNE!' he hollers at last.

27

A Tight Scrape and the Bottom of a Barrel

What do I do? Should I knock everyone out with my bare fists, right now? Isn't that the only way to save Dwayne? I'm looking at my fists – they seem smaller than they once did.

'That no-good mole!' spits Vinny. 'The cats must've got to him! He can't lie, he'd tell them everything!'

'He's a double agent!'

'Let's nail him, boss!'

Vinny waves his hands for silence. 'We can't all be runnin' towards the park as if the Pied Piper's there givin' out free frankfurters. You' – he jabs a finger at one of the rats – 'and you, and you, and you. Come with me. We're gonna knock down some molehills, right now.'

Vinny and his helpers run off and the others break up. At last, only Nev's family and I are left behind the wheelie bins.

'Come on,' sighs Nev's mum, 'let's get home. Right now there's nothing we can do for poor Dwayne. We can't get to the park quicker than the rats.'

'They'll drag him all the way to the sewer, for sure,' says Uncle Alfie. 'We have to think of a plan by then.'

Nev and I are staring at each other. We stay put as the other mice melt away.

All but one of the other mice, that is. Tina has noticed we are hanging back, and is eyeing us suspiciously. 'You two got a better idea?'

Nev and I exchange glances. After her expert spying on the cats at Claude's restaurant, I think Tina might finally have persuaded her brother that she's ready for the big time. Nev sighs. He's given up trying to stop her, at any rate.

'All right,' he says, 'but if you're coming with us you can't tell a soul about it. I mean you *mustn't* breathe a word to anyone, Tina.'

Tina stands up straight. 'I shall be utterly silent.'

'Okay. Good.' Nev takes a deep breath. 'Dwayne isn't in the park.'

Tina's eyes light up. 'He isn't?'

'No. That night we went to talk to him – it wasn't an owl chasing us, it was Francis, spying. I found his feathers stuck to our sweetie bag. That's when we knew Dwayne was in danger.'

'Unfortunately,' I add, 'the alley cats got to him before we did.'

'So where is he now?' asks Tina eagerly.

'In an empty beer keg,' I tell her. 'Right over there.'

We move over to the beer kegs, stopping by the third keg from the left.

'*Dwayne!*' says Nev in a loud whisper. '*Dwayne, it's us!*'

No reply.

'Perhaps it's the wrong barrel,' I suggest.

'Maybe,' says Nev, doubtfully.

Each of us picks a different keg and starts whispering at it.

'*Dwayne?*'

'*Dwaaaayne!*'

'*Dwayne! Dwayne! Dwayne!*'

But Nev is shaking his head. 'We *definitely* left him in that one over there.'

So it's back to the third from the left. Except there's plainly no one inside, so we're standing rather helplessly, looking at it. Suddenly, I notice something on the ground: wet patches, leading away from the barrel. They are roughly the same shape as large flat feet.

'Look,' I say.

'Footprints!' gasps Tina. 'Maybe Dwayne's gone out to look for some grub.'

'But why are his feet wet?' Nev looks anxiously from the prints on the ground to the hole in the side of the beer keg. He scrambles up to peer in the hole, and when he drops back down his eyes are watering. 'It stinks of beer in there.'

'But it's empty,' says Tina.

'Empty yes, but it's not dried out yet. The fumes are really strong ...' Nev blinks hard, shaking his head as if to restore his senses. There is an uneasy pause.

'The footprints are not in the straightest of lines,' I add. Tina puts a hand to her mouth. I think we all know what this means.

We have followed the zigzagging footprints, all the way to the lane on the far side of the Jolly Yachtsman. The good news is this: Dwayne is alive. In fact, he is putting on quite a show. Unfortunately, the *audience* at that show consists of half a dozen alley cats.

'There iss no ffiner thing,' slurs Dwayne, 'than a well-made tuunnel. For goin' about ... ssspying on folks. Now *thass* ... a subtle art ...'

We are watching from atop a pile of crates. Everything about this place spells trouble: the stale smell in the lane; the drip of water into murky puddles; the cat-shaped shadows that creep on the walls.

'An' you should think abou' that,' says Dwayne. '*Sssssubtlety*. Not your ssstrong suit, you lot.'

'No, it ain't,' laughs the big ginger tom. 'We prefer diggin' up your tunnels, don't we Moley?'

The cats snigger.

'Yes! No rrrespect for hard work, you catsss … nnever do any hard work.'

''Course not!' says the smoky grey cat, rolling on to her back. 'We've got stooges to do our spy work for us! Like moles, and pigeons.'

'Ahhh,' says Dwayne, 'pigeons are grubby.'

'Honest as always!' This time it's the black cat with one eye and four white socks. 'You keep that up, Moley. It's the *best policy*.'

'Assolutely. Cannot tell a lie.' Dwayne tries to stand straight and proud, but tips forward.

'Them rats don't know how lucky they are to have you.'

Now they're yowling with laughter.

'Tell us,' says the ginger one, 'how you became so very honest.'

'*Well …*'

Dwayne is really blabbering now, so I'll try to translate …

Okay, so as a young mole, he once … took revenge on some naughty cousins … who played some kind of trick on him with little pieces of earthworms ... by sending them the wrong way through his tunnels ... so that rather than coming up in a field of strawberry plants as he'd said they would, they found themselves ... on a golf course ... surrounded by angry golfers who didn't like moles *or* molehills, and who ... took a swing at them with their golf clubs ...

And the cousins came home ... black and blue. Even for moles. And so great was the shock ... and the row Dwayne got from his parents, and his auntie and his uncle ... that he has never been able to tell a lie since.

The cats are lying down and stretching out, *but also shuffling on their bellies towards Dwayne*, tightening the circle around him.

I am suddenly aware of Tina on my left, preparing to take a daring leap. Nev grabs hold of her.

'Well there's a lesson in there somewhere,' says the tabby, the hugest of them all.

'Sure is,' agrees Dwayne.

'So maybe,' continues the cat, 'we can appeal to that good, honest nature of yours one last time, an' ask if there's one or two itty bitty pieces of information you might not have given us last time we talked.'

'Aaahhh ... tha'll be 'cause you never *asked* lass time we talked.'

'Absolutely. So now we're askin'.' The cat stands up and slinks even closer to Dwayne, but the mole is smiling and swaying gently from side to side. 'Is it true what everyone's sayin' about the hamster? We've been hearin' all about him, this hamster who's got in with the rats. Seems he's makin' quite an impression.'

I feel a little quiver running down my spine. I'm not sure whether it's pride or panic. Tina gives me a thumbs up.

'Is it true he's as big as a guinea pig? That he can toss bicycles and lift a can of treacle in each hand?'

Dwayne is laughing. 'You mean *Rocco*?'

The cat smiles, but he's showing a lot of fangs and there's a growl in his throat. 'What can you tell us about young Rocco, Moley? We'd all like to congratulate him on his achievements. In person.'

I know this is what I've been dreaming of: showdown with the alley cats, Rocco the Incredible takes on the fearsome enemy (and wins). Yet suddenly I feel a bit light-headed. Nev looks as if he's about to be sick, but Tina is pumping her fist like I've already flattened the lot of them.

'Well, I … ssss'pose that sounds like … a nice … nice thing …' Dwayne's voice is fading, and his head keeps nodding forward on to his chest. 'You see the … the thing 'bout Rocco is …'

'Yes?'

'… he *does* tend to … win … every time … 'cause he has a dog … a dog …'

Dwayne flops to the ground, snoring quietly.

'He has a *what*?' spits the tabby. 'A *dog*? How can he have a dog!' He prods Dwayne hard.

'He's passed out,' sighs the grey cat.

'Well he'll be seein' plenty more of us when he wakes up,' says the black-and-white one. 'That last bit's gonna need some explanation.'

'Let's leave him here, he won't be going anywhere in the next hour or so,' growls the tabby. 'I don't know about you lot, but I'm ready for some more of that delicious fish. Let's go see what our new best friend's been pan frying.'

We duck low as the cats troop past our crates. The ginger cat comes last. 'Sweet dreams, Moley,' he calls over his shoulder. 'We'll be seein' ya.'

We sit perfectly still until they're safely out of earshot. Now, at last, I can say what's on my mind.

'*What's he talking about?!* I have a *dog*?! That's either a genius way of convincing them to stay away, or the best reason they'll hear to make getting rid of me their first priority!'

'I think we should try and wake him up,' says Nev. So we hurry over, and Nev's saying, '*Dwayne. Dwayne,*' softly in his ear, but I'm quite keen to give his shoulders a good shake and see if that helps. Suddenly, Dwayne starts murmuring.

'… a dogged deter … determination.'

'Okay,' says Nev. 'I think that explains Rocco's dog.'

'Well, hulloooo,' Dwayne manages. 'Didn't … sssssee you there.'

'You're blind, Dwayne, you don't see *anything*.'

'True. Ahhhhh. Just wait till I tell you how I … just got rid of a load of those cats, N— … Ne—'

Dwayne's head drops back on to the ground. He's snoring loudly.

'All right,' I say. 'Let's get him out of here.'

We pick Dwayne up and carry him back to the beer kegs. He can sleep it off in one of those – one that is completely fume-free.

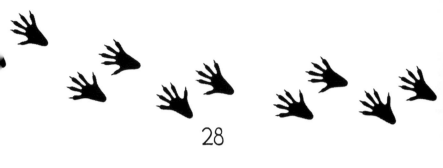

28

Fromage Fray

'How very helpful of them!' Vinny sneers from the front of the chamber. 'Those cats 'ave finally done us a favour by riddin' us of that good-for-nothin' mole. The molehills 'ave been smashed up and the park's a mole-free zone.'

The rats chuckle unpleasantly, but Nev, Tina and I are looking at each other with relief: no one will be looking for Dwayne any longer. Nev's mum and dad, Uncle Alfie and Pip have tears in their eyes, and they're hugging each other, and – oh, yes, of course, they're hugging the three of us as well … I want to tell them right now that Dwayne is fine, but it's too dangerous; it'll have to wait till we're all back at the mouse house.

'All righty,' says Vinny, 'that just leaves us

with the flea-bitten furballs themselves. Not to mention the fiendish cook!'

Cue grunting and muttering from the crowd.

'We are the Big Cheese's gang! We *own* these docks, and there ain't no way we're gonna sit 'ere and wait to be starved out, poisoned, and pounced on like cotton-stuffed cat toys!'

A roar of agreement.

'So what's the plan, boss?' Vinny turns towards the Big Cheese's pipe. 'Is it all-out war, or somethin' more cunning?'

Vinny is rubbing his hands together and is clearly very keen on that second option, but there is silence from the pipe.

'Whatever you say, consider it done! And no messin'!' There are shouts of 'Yeah!' and 'No messin'!' from the other rats.

But still nothing from the Big Cheese.

'Boss? You there, boss?'

Everyone is starting to fidget.

'All right, all right!' Vinny gestures the crowd to be quiet. 'Everyone stay calm. Any bets he's just … just …'

'Just what?'

'Just where?'

'Maybe the villains got to him!' someone squeaks. 'Maybe the Big Cheese is …'

A deathly hush falls over the gang. Vinny thinks about this for a moment.

'Okay,' he says. 'Let's just go knock on his door.'

He scurries out of the chamber and up the pipe that leads to the Big Cheese's private quarters, with everyone hurrying after him. I've never been this way before, although of course I've dreamed of entering the Big Cheese's den. There's a smell like … well, like the smell inside the washing machine the day Gary put me in there with his dirty socks.

Vinny stops by a hole in the wall. On each side of the hole sits a large and particularly plump rat. These are the Big Cheese's personal bodyguards. They are staring at all of us in surprise.

'Where's the boss?' demands Vinny.

One of the guards shrugs. 'Inside, of course,' he says.

'Well he wasn't at the meeting just now. You sure he ain't gone out?'

''Course not. He never goes out, you know that.'

'For reasons of personal security,' adds the other guard.

'And no one else could've slipped in?'

'Like who?'

Vinny eyes them suspiciously. 'How come you pair are still so chubby?'

The two guards look offended.

''Cause you see,' Vinny continues, 'the rest of us 'ave been feelin' a bit peckish lately, lyin' low down 'ere, stayin' out the sight of them cats. You sure you ain't been sneakin' out for snacks? Found a handy stash of grub somewhere and keepin' it all to yourselves? I hope you ain't been bringin' in any titbits for the boss, 'cause you might have heard, there's *poison* doin' the rounds.'

'Look, we ain't been sneakin' no place, 'cause our job is to stand 'ere, like so.'

'And we take our job very seriously.'

'Yes we do. Now why don't *you* try sittin' still, day in, day out, gettin' no exercise or nothin', an' we'll see how the pounds drop off *you*.'

'Fine, fine,' says Vinny impatiently. 'In that case you won't mind all of us goin' into the Big Cheese's office to see he's all right and have a chat with him.'

''Course we'll mind. We're stayin' put, and we ain't lettin' anyone through. Them's the rules.'

'Oh yeah? Well today the rules have changed. You might not let anyone through, but you can't not let *everyone* through.'

The guards barely have time to exchange puzzled glances before the rats pile on top of them. The method of attack seems to be to tip them forward, on to their stomachs. As they rock back and forth on their bulging bellies, they wave all four feet like crazy, but can't make them touch the ground.

So just like that, we're all squeezing through

the hole and racing through the dark passageway that leads to the Big Cheese's chamber. Now everyone's spilling through the doorway … I'm just trying to get in among them, and … *ouch* … I'm being carried through, wedged between several warm, wiry bodies …

Inside the chamber, I'm struck by many things at once. There are makeshift shelves from floor to ceiling, bending under the weight of all kinds of foodstuffs … Then there's the shapeless blob of candle wax over by the far wall, and in the corner, another shapeless blob …

No. Wait. The blob in the corner is a rat, a *huge* rat who makes the guards back at the hole look like little dainty rats … He's lying on his back, snoring at high volume … As a matter of fact, he's lying on an old roller skate with the upper part of the shoe torn off …

'Is that the Big Cheese?'

I didn't mean to say that out loud, but then, someone had to. Everyone is gathered round. There are shocked faces. Disbelieving faces. Angry faces.

'Boss?' says Vinny. The giant rat does not stir. 'BOSS! BOSS! WAKE UP!!'

The Big Cheese wakes with a start, grunting loudly. 'What? What? Who —?' He stares, blinking. 'Woss all this about? You ain't s'posed to be in 'ere.'

'You weren't at the meeting, *boss*,' growls Vinny. 'We was concerned that somethin' bad had happened.'

'Well I'm fine. As you can see. So all of you can clear off back to the chamber and tell me what I missed.'

There is a lot of snarling and shaking of heads.

'Afraid we can't do that, boss,' says Vinny. 'See, all this time we thought you was our upstandin' leader who stays in 'ere for security reasons. But it turns out you ain't upstandin', 'cause you can't even *stand up*, and you've been stayin' in 'ere so that none of us would know what a lazy layabout you are.'

The Big Cheese bristles. 'You criticise me because of my size?' he asks huffily, in a suddenly posh accent.

'No!' Once again I didn't mean that to come out, but there it is; and now everyone's looking at me, so I better continue. 'We criticise you because you are greedy and dishonest! You let others do all the work, find all the food – while you feast on what they bring back!'

I can hear murmurs of agreement all around me, and I'm not done yet.

'You might not have noticed, but we've all been rather hungry lately, since those cats came along. Perhaps you *forgot to mention* your secret store of gourmet grub, or maybe you just don't like to share!'

'*How dare you!!*' explodes the Big Cheese. '*I demand respect!*'

There it is again, the sudden absence of gangster-speak. I point my most accusing finger.

'You, sir, are a fraud! You're not even a gangster, are you?'

The Big Cheese folds his arms. 'I'll have you know that I *led* the rodent invasions of *three* luxury hotels. But you can't go on avoiding those dratted pest controllers forever, you know. And so I was forced to seek out fine cuisine wherever I could get it. Play the part of a dim-witted bully to rise to the top of *this* lot. Do you think I live in this dirty sewer by *choice*?'

The others look offended. Come to think of it, I should be offended too: I *did* choose to live here.

'It's a perfectly nice sewer,' I say.

Everyone turns to stare at me – approvingly. All except the Big Cheese, of course, who clearly wishes he could run me over with his roller skate, and Vinny, who I guess had all of this under control till I opened my big mouth and took over.

Suddenly, the Big Cheese begins laughing crazily. 'You'll never overthrow me!' he squeaks. 'I'm untouchable! I'm unbeatable! I'm too darn big! Haha!'

Tina rushes past me … and begins trying to tip over the Big Cheese's skate.

'What are you doing?' he demands.

In an instant, the three rats standing closest have rushed to assist Tina. Together, they heave the skate on to its edge. The Big Cheese lands on the floor with a heavy thud and a sour face.

'Dirty rats,' he whimpers.

29

The Crowd-pleaser

We stand quietly as the Big-Cheese-No-More exits the sewer. The squeaking of the wheels on his roller skate as it rumbles through the pipe fades gradually, along with his mutterings about the unfairness of it all. Two of the rats have sneaked out behind him, just to make sure he actually leaves.

Finally, there is silence – save a crunching here and a munching there, as more than a few of the gang help themselves to the shelf-loads of goodies.

'All right then,' someone says, 'what happens next?'

'We 'ave to find us a new leader, of course!'

'And fast!'

'Well you needn't look far.' Vinny strides to the front of the group. 'I think it's pretty obvious who the next Big Cheese should be. I've practically been runnin' the show anyhow, ever since we went arms tradin' with the magpies.'

'Yeah, and look how that turned out!' yells a small rat.

'It was the 'amster who saved the day that time!' cries someone else.

'It was the 'amster's fault we got into that mess,' shouts Vinny, his eyes glowing, 'with his nonsense about the foxes selling their patch to some posh Siamese alley cats! And speaking of the foxes, well, they didn't like that rumour very much, now, did they? Nearly got us all killed, so he did!'

'But it was Rocco who found out the cats really *was* comin'. Got it right that time round.'

'*And* he got the cheese out Claude's mousetrap and lived.'

'And don't forget he can knock folks out with bicycles.'

The small room is filled with chattering voices.

'There's only one way to sort this out,' says a tall rat near the front of the crowd. 'Whoever beats the alley cats becomes the new Big Cheese! Tell us, Vinny: what's your plan for kickin' out the kitties?'

All eyes turn to Vinny. He clears his throat and fidgets with his long fingers.

'Ah … well I'm workin' on that, we're *all* workin' on that, ain't we? … If we all gets our heads together …'

There are unhappy mutterings. Now the tall rat is looking at me.

'And what about you, Rocco? What's *your* plan?'

I can feel Vinny's glare drilling through me.

'Well ... the thing is ... I don't really *make* plans, you see. I've found that I'm not much good at them. Usually I just throw myself into the fray, have a flash of inspiration and come out victorious.' As I'm saying all of this, I can feel a change coming over me: something bright and hopeful, washing away the doubt. 'And yes, it's also true that I've had a few mishaps. But I suppose no one ever achieved greatness without a mistake or two along the way, did they? And when you think about it, maybe it's *learning* from your mistakes that makes a truly great leader ... Someone who doesn't give up when things go wrong, but who grows, and becomes wiser, and *better*?'

Everyone is looking at me in silence. 'That's all I can say, really,' I add – and suddenly the room is buzzing, filled with cheering and clapping and whoops of excitement that can only be Tina's.

'Good answer, mate!' says the tall rat. 'A pet 'amster – who'd 'ave thought it?' He and several others are slapping me on the back. 'You, my friend, are just one crazy stunt away from bein' the next Big Cheese!'

I look at Nev; to my surprise, he's giving me two thumbs up. As I think about all of this, a spark of excitement fizzes in my belly. I realise now that what I'm feeling is not a *change* in me, but a *return* to how I used to feel: the same energy, the same buzz, the same certainty that I've got what it takes. After all, didn't I come here to lead, to climb my way to the very top? Isn't this the moment I've been waiting for?

Yes, it is. And do you know what? All of a sudden I am Rocco the Re-energised, ready to lead this gang to victory against cats, chefs, or anyone else who gives us trouble.

'Okay then!' I shout. 'Just give me one day to spy on them! They must have some weakness – the cats and the crazy killer chef – and I swear I'll find it!'

I think Vinny was poised to spring on me just then, but he's been swept aside by a tidal wave of rats all rushing to surround me. Nev's family are hugging me, except Tina, who's punching the air – and I feel exactly like I did that sunny afternoon when I left Gary's house for good. I feel like I'm on the brink of something spectacular.

30

No Light Bulb

I'm spying alone, of course – this is the beginning of my ultimate test, and if I'm to prove that I really should be the next Big Cheese, I have to do this on my own. Tina wasn't too happy about being left out, but I told her that she'll soon have her moment to shine, before all of this is over.

I'm creeping past Chef Claude's back door, because those cats are bound to be around here somewhere. My heart is drumming in my ears, making it pretty hard to hear anything else ... but I'm sure I can make out voices nearby.

Yes, I can. *Cat voices.*

I run to the corner of the building, keeping close in against the wall. Slowly, I poke my head into the lane next to the restaurant.

And there they are, skulking among the

rubbish. I hold my nerve, keep watching. The tabby is pacing up and down, the fur on his back standing on end.

'The mole must've been faking it,' he hisses angrily. 'There's no way he could have sobered up in the time we were gone. He was sober all along.'

The others nod and mutter their agreement. At least, I think that's what they're doing, although I'm not really looking at them any more. My eyes are gathering up every important detail about the scene – such as the little fish-shaped skeletons strewn everywhere. There are so many of those, I'd say the cats must be living here.

Suddenly I sense something: two glimmering green lights, shining through the shadows in the lane …

Eyes!

Looking this way!

I duck back around the corner, out of sight. The cats are still talking, so I risk a quick glance. I can see that the eyes belong to the big ginger cat, now chomping on a fish head. Clearly, he didn't spot me.

Okay. I've got enough information. I turn and scurry back the way I came. I know what you're thinking: I should have hung around longer, to hear what the cats might be plotting. But it was just too risky. Besides, I don't really *care* what the cats are plotting, because *I'm* plotting too. And now I know where they live.

What I need is somewhere quiet to think about my next move. Somewhere far away from Chef Claude's. I think I know just the place.

Perfecto's Pizzeria is redecorating, and half the old fixtures and fittings are piled by its wheelie bins. I dash straight over there, have a quick sniff around. Bingo: a round lampshade, made of thick plastic like fake glass. It's the perfect hiding place. I nestle inside, and get down to thinking …

Okay, so to be honest you're distracting me a tiny bit, because I know *exactly* what you're going to say: that I like being in this lampshade because it reminds me of my old hamster ball back at Gary's. Well, all right then – maybe I'm drawn to something familiar, something that reminds me of the plastic sphere that once protected me from many perils, and allowed me to escape them for all time. This does not mean that I secretly long to return to my life as a pet. I don't know *how* you could suggest such a thing …

All right, calm down, Rocco. Keep thinking. All I have to do is figure out what happens next: how to set the ball in motion, throw myself and the gang into battle. Then the usual chaos and magic and triumph will follow.

All right, so the *figuring out* part is starting to feel a little too much like *making a plan* – never my strong point – and is certainly taking longer than expected. To be fair, I'm being horribly put off by some very noisy dogs, who're playing with a squeaky toy while their owners have a picnic on the grass behind the new flats …

If I can just focus … and if they can all stop barking and yelping for one—

Shhhh. Wait a minute. I can hear something else, like fast little footsteps. Someone's coming.

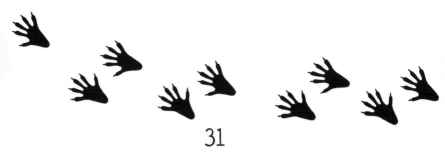

31

Bottled Up

Now before I tell you this, you must promise that you won't panic. It's going to sound really bad – that's true – but by now *really bad* has become a speciality of mine. I can deal with it. I'm fantastic, remember? Everyone's saying it now. One last, brilliant victory and I'll be the new Big Cheese, so I know I can handle this …

Oh, all right. Here's what it is.

It was a couple of rats who were coming … coming to tell me they've found Dwayne.

They heard his snoring, echoing inside that empty beer keg. So they pulled him out, and carried him down the bank, and stuck his head in the river to wake him up. He picked up right where he had left off, and finished the sentence he was trying to get his tongue around when he passed out …

The one that ended with 'Nev'.

So now the rats have Dwayne *and* Nev locked up in a brandy bottle, and they're very keen that I should come and decide what's to be done about all this.

Right now, I'm staring after the eager pair of fellows who found him, those bearers of bad news, as they hurry away, racing back towards the sewer.

There's nothing else for it, so I tear after them all the way back to the gang's lair, and down, down into its darkest depths. We come upon a crowd of rats, jostling and jabbering and blocking our path. One of the rats who brought me here whistles, and the crowd parts to let me through. I scurry to the front as quick as I can …

… and feel a sinking sensation in my stomach. Nev's hands are pressed against the side of the brandy bottle. He's staring out at me in desperation. I'm mouthing the words, '*DON'T WORRY*,' but for some reason he only seems to look more worried. Dwayne is sitting next to him, looking utterly miserable.

I turn to face the rats. I sit up on my back legs to make myself look tall, or make myself *feel* tall … They're pressing forward and sneering, showing lots of crooked teeth.

'All right then,' I say. 'So it turns out the cats didn't rid us of disloyal Dwayne! And so he escaped, aided by this untrustworthy Nev— I mean, untrustworthy mouse. Do we, um … do we know anything else?'

'Yeah,' says Vinny, 'we know the mouse is so desperate for mercy that he confessed straight away. Spilled his guts, so he did. Told us how he helped the mole escape the park and stashed him in the beer barrel for safe-keeping.'

I am suddenly aware of the other mice, standing to the left of the bottle. Nev's family are plainly terrified – except for Tina, who is bubbling with fury and miming something I can't quite understand. She is making chopping motions with one hand and slicing motions with the other. I believe she's showing me the violent action she thinks we should take. I shake my head at her to make her stop.

'Told us right away,' Vinny says again. ' "It was me, you got me. No one else knew a thing." We didn't even have to threaten him – he just cracked! What a coward.'

'Actually, I think that was rather brave.' *Where did that come from?! Get a grip, Rocco!* 'Not that that excuses this treachery, or … makes it any less … um … severely punishable …'

I hear the sound of Nev's head thudding against the glass as he slumps in despair.

'So what do we do now, Rocco?' someone asks. 'Do we beat them up? Chop them up?'

197

The rats cheer.

'Throw them to the alley cats?'

A bigger cheer.

'Chuck the bottle out to sea?'

A *wild* cheer.

'No!' They all stare at me in surprise. 'None of those! I mean … all those things are – far too soft!' There are murmurs of approval. 'But we don't have time right now to be nearly as nasty as we should be! There are cats to be getting rid of, not to mention the demon chef! First we have to crush *them*, before they think up some other, even fouler trick than dodgy meatballs! Then we can deal with, you know … this …'

I wave vaguely in the direction of the brandy bottle. From the nodding of heads, it seems that this is a popular idea. I risk a wink at Nev's family, but they don't look any less anxious. Tina is miming again so I quickly look away, and as I do so I meet Nev's gaze. Both he and Dwayne are lying low inside the bottle – but suddenly I can see hope in Nev's eyes … relief, I think, that I've at least bought us some time.

'So what do we do, Rocco?'

'How do we crush them cats?'

'Let's have it, Rocco,' sneers Vinny. 'Share your little *flash of inspiration*.'

I squeeze my eyes tight shut. Everything I've seen and heard lately is streaming through my mind like a crazy film show …

… with a constant flashing image of Nev and Dwayne, trapped in a brandy bottle …

THINK, Rocco. Come on …

Divert rats. Attack cats. Rescue Nev and Dwayne … the unstoppably honest Dwayne …

'Rocco does tend to win …'

Yes I do. I do.

'… 'cause he has a dog … a dog …'

Noisy dogs playing, me in my lampshade, couldn't think straight …

I wish I was back there, in my lampshade … shade, shield, hamster ball, wonderful sphere of protection from peril … from Gary's dog, Gary's cat …

Cats. Alley cats! Focus, Rocco.

Fish bones. Lane. Fish bones.

Yes, but how to set the ball in motion …?

How to set the –

My eyes are wide open.

'I'VE GOT IT!'

Everyone jumps, me included – I almost forgot they're all standing there.

'I know exactly what we have to do,' I tell them. 'Those cats are gonna be completely bowled over!'

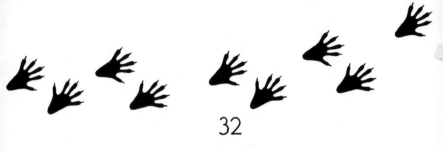

32

Dog Gone

Behind the Jolly Yachtsman: me, Tina, and two rats who've helped push the Secret Weapon over here from Perfecto's Pizzeria.

The Secret Weapon. That's what I'm now calling the round plastic lampshade.

I step inside the shade. It's made to look like frosted glass, so all I can see through it is a blur of light and colour. I'll need someone to act as my eyes outside – and that's where my specially chosen, special agent Tina comes in. Of course, I have to pretend that I'm *forcing* her to help out; after all, the rats think I'm planning to kill her big brother. So I'd better sound suitably mean.

'Right you,' I tell her, 'listen up! Give me a yell if I'm building too much speed.'

'Roger that.'

'All right then.' I take a deep breath. 'Let's go.'

'Good luck, boss!' shout the two rats.

Boss. With that amazing syllable still ringing in my ears, I reach high up the inside of the lampshade, lean my full weight against it … and start to roll. Tina's toenails tap on the cobbles as she runs alongside. 'Great start, Rocco! All clear to the end of the lane!'

I'm picking up speed. The shade is a lot heavier than my hamster ball.

'End of the lane comin' up!' shouts Tina. 'Go left, left!'

I lean left – the shade responds nicely. I feel totally in control. 'You okay to pick up the pace a bit, Tina?'

'Absolutely! I've got tons in the tank!'

'Then let's see what this thing can do!'

We're running now as fast as we can. Me driving, Tina giving directions.

Along the empty road to the old warehouse. *Left.*

Down past the brewery, weaving our way through a maze of wooden crates. *Right.*

Following the water's edge, all the way to the little footbridge … up, up, and over the bridge.

All the while avoiding the streets, busy with humans.

But Tina's transport references are becoming harder to follow.

'Bank to the nearside!'

'The what?'

'Left! Go left!'

I swerve to the left.

'Salty's Seafood Bistro, twelve o'clock! Hard to starboard!'

'*What?!*'

'Reverse thrust! RUDDER, ROCCO, RUDDER!'

I take a guess, make another sharp turn to the left.

'Noooo!' cries Tina.

Too late. I'm —

OH! AH! WHOA! BOUNCING! — DOWN! — STEPS!!

Uuuugghhh. I feel sick, and I'd swear there was a nasty cracking sound just then as the ball, I mean shade, I mean Secret Weapon landed at the bottom of those evil stone steps. Tina grabbed on just as the shade began to tumble, and is now hanging from the opening at the top. 'Genius, Rocco! Your route was quicker, and so much more fun!'

Sure enough, the sound of barking tells me that Tina and I have ended up on the very same patch of grass that we set out for. Somewhere up ahead, as their owners enjoy a picnic under the skinny trees behind the flats, half a dozen dogs are still in a frenzy over a squeaky toy.

As always, I have masterminded a happy accident.

'Okay!' I cry. 'You ready for this?'

'No kiddin'!'

We're off again, heading straight for the dogs. I'm a little worried by the deep crack running halfway around the shade, but I'm sure it'll be just fine.

'Veer left!' says Tina. 'Let's get the German shepherd's attention!'

I like her thinking. I veer to the left.

'All right! He's lookin' at us. He's dropped the toy!'

'Good stuff. What's he doing now? Should I keep getting closer?'

'No. Stop a minute.'

I stop. I wait a minute. Tina's gone quiet. I risk a whisper: 'Is he coming?'

'Ssshhh! Yes! They're *all* coming!'

By staring as hard as I can through the frosted plastic, I can make out the dogs' blurry, looming figures.

'Don't move!' whispers Tina. 'I'm gonna climb on to the shih-tzu. I'll give you a shout once I'm on board.'

Suddenly it's gone dark. Like my shade is in the shade … or shadow. I can hear a lot of sniffing. Without moving a muscle – save for the ones attached to my eyeballs – I glance to the left.

203

Through the hole in the base of the shade, I can see a big, black, wet nose with flaring nostrils. It's the German shepherd. As the nose presses through the hole and takes a particularly deep snuffle, it is pushed aside by a different nose. They are jostling for position – the German shepherd, the Labrador, the two spaniels.

I look to the right, through the hole at what used to be the top of the lampshade. I can see a whippet a short way across the grass, staring right in at me. She's crouched low, waggling her hindquarters as if poised to pounce.

Where are you Tina?! Where's the shih-tzu?!

Something grey, white and hairy trots into view and, thankfully, comes to a halt between me and the whippet. It's the shih-tzu, looking confused. And there's the reason why: Tina is dangling from his silky locks. Now she's scrambling up, towards his shoulder …

She's done it! I can see her, right behind his ears, clinging on to the little red ribbon in his hair. And from the way he's hurrying over here with a surprised look on his face, I'd say she's steering him, too. Yes! I can see her little hands pushing his ponytail forward like a joystick.

The shih-tzu's big fluffy paw stops right in front of the hole in the lampshade. Now he's ducked down to stare through it, and his eyes are round with shock and bewilderment.

'RUN, ROCCO!' yells Tina. 'GO STRAIGHT AHEAD!!'

I hurl my weight against the shade. I'm struggling to build up speed, because everyone keeps pawing at me ... I can feel the dogs' hot breath as they sniff harder than ever.

Someone knocks me – I'm spinning off course! I run hard, sliding on the slippery plastic – and, phew, I think I've recovered.

'SPOT ON, ROCCO!' shouts Tina. 'JUST KEEP GOING!'

The dogs might have been wary at first, but now they're enjoying themselves, yapping and springing around the lampshade. Once, twice, three times, some hairy snout or another slams into me – but I keep going, barging on through, refusing to lose my way! I am Rocco the Steadfast!

'HOW ARE WE DOING?!' I yell.

'GREAT! WE'RE NEARLY OFF THE GRASS! THEN IT'S ALL DOWNHILL!'

I make a final push, and suddenly the shade is rumbling fast along the footpath. Now I'm in complete control ...

Well, almost. We're picking up speed here – Tina was right about going downhill.

Still getting faster.

And faster ... oh, help, *too much speed*!

The dogs are barking like crazy; if Tina's

shouting instructions I'll never hear. I'm tearing along this path like a rocket, but they're *right behind me* …

Impossibly, the shade is still building speed. I can't— run fast enough, my— feet can't get a grip … I'm going to—

AAAHHH!! I'm spinning! I'm pinned against the plastic! … Ohhhhh, my head, it's just like the day Gary put me in the tumble dryer …

Wait … I think the ground's levelled off … Yes. Yes, don't panic, I've almost got it back under control … but, oh, I feel dizzy …

'RIGHT!' screams Tina.

The inside of the shade is whirling before my eyes, but I lean to what I'm hoping is the right-hand side …

'PERFECT!'

Oh good.

Oh no. The nasty crack the shade suffered when it fell down the steps is growing. Worse still, there's a whole spider's web of little cracks spreading out from it.

This thing's gonna break.

'HOW MUCH FURTHER?!' I pant.

'NOT FAR NOW! WE'RE ON THE MAIN STREET ALREADY!'

'WE'RE ON THE *WHAT*??!!'

I know I heard Tina correctly, because over all the barking I can hear people screaming. I can see the shapes of their feet and legs as they dive out the way of the crazed dogs.

I keep going ... rushing straight into Tina-knows-what ...

Another BUMP ... another crack! ... Did I just drop off the kerb? *Am I on the road?* A rush of engine noise and a shadow flitting overhead tell me that *yes, I am on the road and I just bowled my way between the wheels of a large vehicle.*

'TINA —! Oomph!'

I think I just bumped on to the pavement at the other side. I'm going to assume that none of the dogs has been flattened.

Suddenly, the spidery cracks are tearing in all directions around the sphere – I'm staring at an eye-watering jigsaw of tiny pieces, desperate to fall apart ...

'CHEF CLAUDE'S A-COMIN' UP!' whoops Tina.

Not soon enough, not soon enough ...

'PREPARE TO SWING A RIGHT!'

'I'M READY! I'M READY!'

I can hear it cracking, I can —

'NOWWWW!!!'

I throw myself to the right. This must be it – the lane next to Claude's. I'm bouncing over fish bones – I'm —

SMASH.

I'm sitting in a daze, surrounded by pieces of

broken lampshade. The dogs leap over me – and keep going. Tina lets go of the shih-tzu and lands perfectly, between two razor-sharp fragments.

'Kitties at twelve o'clock,' she whispers, a dangerous gleam in her eyes.

I look up. As the six dogs hurtle towards them, I've just enough time to take in those flabbergasted feline faces – and all of them are staring at *me*.

'ALLOW ME TO INTRODUCE MYSELF!' I holler. 'MY NAME IS ROCCO! AND THESE HERE ARE MY DOGS! *PLURAL!!*'

The cats hiss and spit – but they know they're beaten. They spring from the bins and stacks of rubbish they've been sitting on, and flee down the lane as the dogs give chase. Mad barking echoes off the walls, making our half-dozen pets sound like a pack of wild coyotes.

Tina and I run after them, all the way to the end of the lane. Here, behind the restaurants, we are looking down into the docks through the haze of late afternoon sun. We watch as the would-be invaders and the happy canines grow smaller and smaller. They fade into frantic dots that are finally lost against the sparkling water.

'Well, Tina,' I say, 'I think that bit's taken care of.'

'Too right.'

We've just done what we've both been dreaming of, and taken down the alley cats. But

I know Tina's thoughts, like mine, have already turned to unfinished business at Claude's bistro.

As we scurry past the lane, towards the back of the restaurant, we can see the cats' fishy leftovers will not be going to waste. For one day at least, the seagulls have found themselves a proper source of grub.

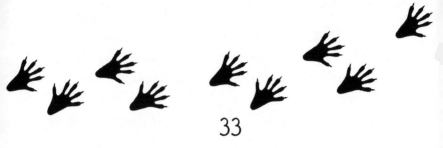

33

Le Riot

The rats and mice are gathered by the back door of Chef Claude's restaurant, eagerly awaiting our arrival.

'The feline foes have gone!' I cry. 'We won't be seeing their mangy faces again anytime soon!'

Cue lots of loud cheering. Even Vinny looks pleased. The mice run towards Tina, but are careful to keep their distance from me. After all, as far as the rats are concerned, I'm the *ruthless boss* who plans to punish Nev and Dwayne.

'Now let's show Monsieur Meatballs his goose is cooked – but not how he likes it!'

Everyone sniggers as they turn towards the kitchen. It's been a hot day, and the back door has been wedged open. 'Thank you Claude,' I murmur as the rats begin to pour through.

The mice and I scurry inside just as Claude's cooks realise what's going on. They grab their meat cleavers and call out wildly, but seem too horrified to actually do anything. Claude hurries in from the store cupboard carrying a box of leeks. He drops it to the floor.

'*Sacré bleu!*' he screams. 'Stop zem, you idiots! Before zey get into *le restaurant!*'

Too late.

As one, the whole lot of us – rats, mice and hamster – slam into the swing doors. *Oomph!* They swing open, and the onslaught begins.

The restaurant is packed. The rats spread out and tear across the floor. One woman is pointing frantically, the blood drained from her face.

'RATS!!'

Now everyone is screaming, leaping out of their chairs or on to their chairs as the rats scramble up the tablecloths.

Chef Claude bursts through the swing doors, waving a carving knife in one hand, a rolling pin in the other. As he bounces around the restaurant, stabbing tabletops and smashing wine glasses, the screaming gets louder. Desperate diners fight to get out the door, as rodent gangsters sink long yellow teeth into their ankles.

Claude keeps yelling something untranslatable. He's throwing over his own tables just to get the rats off them, but they aren't taking any notice. Everyone is completely focused on gathering mouthfuls, no, *armfuls* of food. In fact, there's so much of it lying around that Vinny is leading a small team of sharpshooters in gathering up some of the deadlier items – mussels, black olives, profiteroles – and hurling them at Claude's reddening face.

I'm suddenly aware that I'm standing with Tina and the rest of Nev's family – but the rats are far too busy to notice. I'm also wondering where those other chefs have got to. I glance up at the kitchen doors behind us. Four terrified faces are pressed against the little round windows. I can safely say they've no intention of coming through; but then, there's no harm in making sure, especially when there's so much fun to be had. So I grab a juicy big scallop and lob it at the nearest window. The four faces duck out of sight. Tina and I give each other a high five.

'Uh-oh,' breathes Pip. 'Look out, Rocco.'

I spin around to find a man – tousled and food-splattered – tiptoeing towards me. He has a crazy determined look in his eyes, and his hands are outstretched.

I flatten myself to the floor, showing him my gaping jaws and sharp teeth. *So, fiend, you plan to seize hold of me, but see, your soft pink fingers will not withstand my fearsome –*

Wait a minute. Who is this, stepping out from behind him? I now see this man is working for someone! It's a *child*! A boy, just like Gary ... Maybe skinnier, but no less evil.

'Get him, Daddy, get him!' shouts the evil boy.

But I've an assistant of my own.

'Tina!' I cry. She's already at my side. 'I'll deal with the tiny terror! Now show his dad your four-footed scissor jabs!'

'Right on!'

Tina springs. The man lunges. As he feebly makes a grab at me, I simply dodge to one side.

Tina races up his trouser leg. He's screaming and hopping around – she's unleashing all her martial arts moves, right behind his knee. Now he's waving his leg around frantically. He's trying to shake her out, but the other mice are already pounding him with low-flying chunks of cheese.

I turn my attention to the smaller foe: my arch-enemy. He is creeping towards me with a greedy look on his face.

Come on then, you pint-sized halfwit. I've learned a few new tricks since the last time I outsmarted the likes of you.

He makes a dive.

I run between his grubby sneakers: piece of cake.

He's chasing me, of course. 'Hamster! Hamster!' he yells. 'Come back!'

Come back?! Do you think I have a tiny brain?

He attempts a snatch! I slip easily through his bony fingers.

But that's enough already – it's time to shut this criminal down. I'm looking for inspiration as I dart this way and that.

I see chairs lying everywhere ... upturned tables, tablecloths, puddles of red wine ... I'm running between rats, rats carrying food, rats chasing screeching diners ... weaving between the diners' feet, but I can't seem to lose him, I can hear him giggling right behind me ...

Splattered soup, half-eaten chicken, breadsticks ...

Breadsticks! That's it!

I am reminded of a magical moment: a cocktail stick, a bicycle chained to a railing, a couple of squished rats!

I turn sharply, almost running back the way I came. Ha! He didn't see *that* coming, and now he's standing stupidly, staring after me. I've already got a breadstick in my hands. That's right – I'm grasping it at one end ...

And now I'm running with it, two-legged style ... straight towards the nasty boy, whose mouth is open.

That's right! You'd BETTER turn and run!

At last, it is I who gives chase! And here's just what I need, coming right up – a squashed éclair! I drop the far end of my breadstick into the cream —

It sticks!

Just like that day in the lane: a perfect pole vault, and here I am – hanging on to the scoundrel's shorts! He's swatting at me, but I've already climbed up his back pocket.

'THIS IS FOR ALL THE POCKET-MONEY PETS!' I cry.

I sink my teeth deep into my enemy's rump.

'AAAAHHHH!! DADDYYYY!!'

I drop to the floor.

I chuck an olive at him as he runs for the door. It smacks him on his nibbled rear.

His dad runs past me, also fleeing for the door. I'm suddenly reminded of Tina. Now I'm racing back towards the kitchen – but of course, I needn't have feared. Tina is standing with the other mice. She salutes me.

'Tina,' I tell her, 'you are a martial arts hero at last.'

'And *you've* just started the rebellion!' she declares. 'Imprisoned rodents everywhere will be freed from their human captors!'

I like that – but it sounds like a mission for another day. And so at last, we begin to eat. As I take my first mouthful of omelette, delicately sprinkled with something green, I'm suddenly aware of how hungry I am. We munch on trampled crêpes and squashed cheese, crumbs of baguette and flecks of soufflé.

As for Chef Claude, he's shouting and screaming, and – ah – flinging a wine bottle at Vinny and the crack shots ...

SMASH.

There goes the front window. He seems very determined to destroy his own restaurant, but I suspect it's the health inspector who'll finish the job.

34

The New Big Cheese

I am standing atop Minestroni's old brick.

'Let's hear it for the new Big Cheese!' someone hollers.

'HOORAAAH!' comes the chorus, amid loud applause.

'First Big Cheese we've ever 'ad who got there by doin' some good, 'stead of by murd'rin' folks,' says a rat at the front of the crowd.

Everyone presses closer to my brick, arms outstretched.

'C'mon boss! Jump!'

I close my eyes and jump. Now I'm being passed around the crowd, held high while everyone chants my name. This is my moment, at long last. Everybody wants to follow me, to be just like me, to conquer the world with me.

As my feet finally touch the floor, I turn to face my merry gang.

'Thank you!' I cry. 'The hard part is over. We've found our true courage. Now it's up to each one of us how we use it. But first, let's party.'

Of course, the rats need no such invitation. As I stand here, watching them laughing and stuffing themselves with gourmet goodies, picking fights over the tastiest ones, I can feel a lump in my throat. Isn't this all I've ever wanted?

Not quite. There's something else.

No one is paying the slightest bit of attention, so I slip from the chamber and steal along the pipe, all the way to the mouse house.

Nev's family are waiting.

'All right,' I tell them, 'the party is young. I'd say the timing's about right.'

'Thanks Rocco,' says Nev's dad. 'Just keep an eye out, make sure no one leaves the chamber for at least the next ten minutes. That should give us enough time to get Nev and Dwayne out of that bottle and make our way to the surface.'

'The old Big Cheese's bodyguards are on duty, guarding the bottle,' adds Uncle Alfie. 'We're taking the teaspoon to knock them out.'

'Have no fear,' says Tina, boxing the air. 'I'll take care of those two.'

'And a fine job you'd do too, Tina,' I tell her, 'but I can't let you. You see, there's a much safer way to get past them.' Everyone looks at me, confused. 'Someone's got to tell them to go join the party.'

'But they won't take orders from anyone except the Big Cheese,' says Pip. 'And that means you.'

'Exactly. I have to go down there and send them on their way. If they see Nev's own family coming, they'll know it's a rescue mission – but not so if it's just me.'

'No Rocco!' cries Tina. 'What are you saying? If you do that everyone'll know *you're* the one who rescued Nev and Dwayne!'

'Probably.'

'But that means you won't get to be Big Cheese any more! They'll be after *your* blood! Again!'

'It's all true.'

Tina seems to shrink before my eyes. Her fur is matted with tears. 'But you wanted to be a great leader,' she whispers. 'You can't give that up now.'

I shrug. I was practising my *not-too-bothered* face before the party – but you know, now it comes to it … even though it hurts to achieve my dream and then give it all up again, I know it's the right thing to do. So I'm really *not* too bothered after all.

'Nev and Dwayne are in trouble,' I say. 'That's all that matters now. I know all of you would face any danger for them, but I can't just stand by and not help. And besides … I think there's a different kind of gang I'd rather be a member of.'

Wow. Another new emotion is welling up inside me … No, actually it's not so new; I felt this before, a long time ago. It feels warm, and kind of safe.

Tina wipes her eyes. 'Our mousy family gang?' she asks.

'Exactly.'

The mice surround me in a group hug. And now I remember: my mother, my brothers and sisters, curled up close before we were separated forever. *This* is how it feels to be loved – not just adored for what you've done, or the reputation you've got, but loved for being *you*, no matter what. Maybe this is what I've been searching for, and I didn't even know it. I wanted to *belong*, and now I do. Now I really do.

'Oh Rocco,' sighs Nev's mum, 'I'm sorry for ever saying you were a liability.' I don't remember her saying that, but never mind. 'You're an extraordinary, inspiring hamster – any sewer rat can see that – but you know what real courage is all about: doing the right thing and doing it for others. That's what makes you so brave. I'm so proud to have you as the newest member of our family.'

'Hear hear,' says Nev's dad.

The lump is back in my throat, and is threatening

to choke me. But we're not out of danger yet, and I just hope I've kept some of that extraordinary inspirational braveness in reserve …

Just kidding – you know me by now.

'Okay,' I tell them, 'meet me – I mean *us* – under the bridge in five minutes.'

'You got it.' Tina makes a fist. 'Let's do this thing.'

'Go quick, Rocco,' says Nev's dad, 'before anyone notices you've left the chamber.'

I nod, and do exactly as he suggests.

35

Rocco the Reinvented (But Still Fantastic)

I stomp along the pipe towards the two huge guards. In the light from the stump of candle in front of them, I can see they look nervous.

'My friends!' I laugh, but with a menacing edge, hopefully. 'Why are you still standing here? The party's up there!' I point back up the pipe. 'There's fancy food and all sorts!'

'But, boss, what about—'

'Guarding that bottle?' I wave a hand dismissively. 'I'll take a turn! I intend to be a hands-on leader, so why not start now? Besides, I haven't had a chance to *speak personally* with our two mischief-makers! As in make horrible threats, hahaha!'

The guards are clearly desperate to accept my offer. 'Yeah, sure thing, boss. You're the boss an' all.'

'Yes I am! And *you* look like you could use a snack!'

The pair waddle up the pipe as fast as they are able. As I hurry towards the bottle I can see Nev and Dwayne lying inside. Nev is waving weakly.

'Give me two seconds!' I say.

I unscrew the cap with both hands, and as it drops off Nev sticks out his head and gasps for breath. Quickly he slides out of the bottle. 'Thank you Rocco!' He looks confused. 'But what are you doing here? The guards told us the cats are gone and you're the new Big Cheese.'

'I sure am. Which I figure is pretty much everything I set out to achieve here, so there's no point in hanging around. Now is there room for one more in your escape party or not?'

Nev looks at me like he wants to say something but can't think of the words. 'Of course there is,' he says instead. Now he's smiling. 'You know Rocco, you might be just a little bit nuts, but you're the best friend any mouse could ask for.'

I feel a warm glow in my chest as I smile right back. We turn to check on Dwayne. The mole is wriggling for all he's worth, trying to squeeze himself out of the bottle. 'This is what comes,' he gasps, 'of being so luxuriantly velvety!'

I would suggest that it has more to do with eating a few too many earthworms, but we've no time to discuss it. Nev takes hold of Dwayne's big hands and pulls. I put my arms around Nev's middle, and we heave, *once … twice …* I'm beginning to wonder how the rats shoved him in there in the first place … *three times …*

Pop.

Nev and I fall backwards, with Dwayne landing on top. 'Thank you,' he says.

We pick ourselves up and make for the exit, tiptoeing quickly through the pipe. As we draw closer to the chamber, we slow down … the sounds of the party are all but gone. With all that food in their bellies, the rats must have fallen asleep. Finally, nothing stands between us and the light of the setting sun.

We run. My heart's beating faster, I'm growing lighter with every bound …

Almost there … racing straight for the circle of light at the end of the tunnel …

We spill through the front door – *and are met by grinning faces*. Not mouse faces.

We skid to a halt, face to face with a crooked face.

A possibly mad, worryingly gleeful face.

Vinny's face.

I'm staring straight into his bloodshot eyes. Dwayne sniffs the air and groans.

'Well what's this?' squeaks Vinny. 'Fancy meetin' you 'ere. The Big Cheese 'imself, doin' a runner with his traichous ... traitous ...'

'Traitorous?' I suggest.

Vinny nods. '... friends. Methinks it's time to make a Big Cheese sandwich out of your cold dead corpses.'

Vinny is standing with the old Big Cheese's bodyguards, along with half a dozen other rats. There is no sign of Nev's family.

'Actually,' I try, 'I was just about to chuck these two into the river, as soon as I had bitten off all their little fingers.'

'Ha!' spits Vinny. 'There ain't no lie can get you out of this one, hamster. I heard what you was plottin' with them mice.'

'You did?' Oops.

'Every dirty detail 'bout how you'd rescue these double-crossin' runts and bail out on us. Didn't you notice I skipped your little party back there?'

The simple answer would be *no*.

'Well you never did like me very much.'

'Quite so. Ha! As if I'd be raisin' a toast to some kiddie's pet takin' over this gang. But more than that, I knew you'd be up to no good – knew it in me bones – so I hid out in them pipes, and I heard it all. Then all I had to do was stop these stooges in their tracks' – he points at the two guards – 'and gather up everyone who wasn't too overstuffed to come up 'ere and lie in wait for ya.'

Actually, I'm not so sure that *anyone* isn't too overstuffed. All the rats are weighed down by bulging stomachs, including Vinny, who clearly took a few snacks with him when he hid in the pipes.

'It's a pity that you are all full up, and slow,' I say, and I'm giving Nev a poke behind my back at this point, 'otherwise I would give you a most painful reminder of how I came to be Big Cheese in the first place.' Now I'm using two fingers – still behind my back – to imitate a pair of little fast-running legs. From the way he just squeezed my hand, I'd say Nev wholeheartedly agrees with this course of action. 'But since you are all fat and helpless, it would not be fair. And I always fight fair.'

Vinny laughs loudly, and now the fingers behind my back are tiptoeing.

'Let's see you try,' he yells, looking poised to jump on us, ''cause as a matter of fact we're just about *helpless* enough to squash the three of you into pâté!'

'*NOT so very FAST!*'

We turn quickly to stare at the top of the embankment. There, under the shadow of the bridge, is the Big Cheese – I mean, the former Big Cheese. He's sitting atop his roller skate looking extremely angry. And standing right behind him are none other than Nev's family.

'You are fools! The whole lot of you! Brainless, blundering *fools!*'

'What you on about?' shouts Vinny. 'No one ain't listenin' to you! You've been ousted!'

The ex-Big Cheese is shaking both his fists. 'How dare you! Don't you see what you have done? *You have closed Claude's bistro down!* It is *shut*, and it will *remain* shut, thanks to you and your little *food fight!*'

Vinny and the other rats gasp in horror.

'So you see,' continues the one-time Big Cheese, '*I'll* be the one doing the squashing around here! For the love of French cuisine, I shall leave tyre tracks on your swollen bellies!'

He signals to the mice, who, as one, give the roller skate a good push.

Now the roller skate, complete with enormous rat, is tearing down the embankment.

'RAAAAAAHHHHH!!' cries the ex-Big Cheese.

The world has gone into slow motion. Vinny and the two bodyguards reach out their arms as if to ward off the roller skate, their jaws dropping in horror. The bleary eyes of the other rats seem to gradually open wide.

Nev and I perform a giant, leaping sidestep … taking a bewildered Dwayne with us …

But the rats are less light on their feet.

The old Big Cheese knocks his bodyguards over like skittles – smacks into Vinny – now Vinny's in the river and the roller skate is upside down, wheels spinning in the air. The former boss rat and his two guards land squarely on top of two party-goers each, pinning the lot of them down.

Vinny is doing a lot of splashing. 'GET ME OUT OF HERE!' He keeps disappearing under the water then popping up again. 'YOU IDIOTS! DON'T— JUST STAND THERE!'

Nev's family reach the bottom of the bank.

'Thank you, all of you!' says Dwayne. Nev is hugging his little sister.

'That,' I add, 'was inspired.'

Now Tina, Nev and I are looking at each other.

'Roller skate,' we say together.

All eight of us take hold of the skate, and flip it back on to its wheels.

'Just what … do you think you're doing?' murmurs its dazed owner.

Everyone scrambles on board, except Uncle Alfie and me.

'DON'T YOU— EVEN THINK ABOUT IT!' gasps Vinny, still splashing desperately. 'STAY RIGHT— WHERE YOU ARE!'

'Not likely,' mutters Nev.

'But Vinny,' I shout, 'with me gone, you'll get to be Big Cheese! Isn't that good news?'

'TOO— RIGHT!' he gurgles. 'I *WILL* BE BIG—CHEESE!— AND HERE'S WHAT I'M— GONNA DO!'

At that, there is a familiar fluttering of wings. Francis descends out of nowhere, clutching Vinny by his shoulders and keeping his head above the water. Clearly, the ever-present spy would like to hear *exactly* what the next Big Cheese is going to do.

'I'M GONNA KILL YOU!'

No surprises there, then. Uncle Alfie and I begin to shove the roller skate. The others each push one foot against the ground, and we're off.

'I'M GONNA KNOCK DOWN EVERY PET SHOP IN THIS CITY JUST TO MAKE SURE THERE AIN'T ANOTHER ONE OF YOU!'

Uncle Alfie and I hop on to the skate.

'COME BACK 'ERE!'

Looking over my shoulder, I don't think I'll ever forget this image of a spluttering rat being held at the water's surface by a desperately flapping pigeon.

I give him a wave, to show that there are no hard feelings.

'JUST YOU WAIT TILL I'VE— DIGESTED—'

Vinny's voice fades out of earshot. I feel a tiny bit rude for hurrying off while he's in the middle of threatening me … Okay, I'm over that now.

The roller skate is speeding along nicely. Tina

is riding up front, whooping and punching the air.

But the embankment is shallower here and there are people up on the pavement. So we bring our trusty transport to a halt and hop off, safely hidden behind a litter bin.

Now we're all standing in silence, catching our breath, just looking at each other.

'I'm sorry things worked out this way,' says Nev. 'I know how much it meant to you to become the Big Cheese, and you deserved it, Rocco.'

I find myself shrugging. 'I always believed I'd be a superstar action hamster. And it's turned out to be so. But I guess there's no point in any of that unless it means doing some good. Not just chasing glory, but helping out my friends. I think, from the moment I left Gary's, all I really had to do was find out who those are.'

'You're the bravest kind of hamster there is, Rocco,' says Tina.

'And there are a lot of things I couldn't have done without some other seriously courageous rodents.'

Nev's little sister is grinning from ear to ear.

'So what do we do now?' asks Pip.

It seems everything's back to normal, because I don't know about the others, but I have no plan whatsoever.

'How about,' says Nev, with a sly smile, 'we

throw ourselves into goodness-knows-what, have a flash of inspiration, and somehow become the most amazingly awesome rodents in the city?'

'Sounds good,' says Nev's mum.

'Then let's randomly choose which way to go,' says Nev's dad. 'Dwayne, since your eyesight's so poor, I'd say you're the perfect mole for the job.'

'Oh … I suppose so.' Dwayne hesitates, then points to the left.

We run along the water's edge with the evening sun in our eyes. I've no idea where we're going, but so long as we stick together we can never fail. I am Rocco the Unstoppable, Rocco the Honorary Mouse, and I've never felt better in my life.

ACKNOWLEDGEMENTS

A big thanks to the creative writing tutors and mentors who've supported me along the way since I first hatched the crazy plan of becoming a writer, and who've always convinced me that I had to keep going.

I'm also ever grateful to the folks at Strathkelvin Writers' Group for friendship, feedback and help, not to mention that all-important sense of togetherness. And to the children who commented on the story for me: hearing how much you enjoyed it has been the best source of encouragement I could have wished for.

Special thanks to Dave Hill for his fantastic cover artwork, and to the team at Matador for all their input.

And last but by no means least, an extra big thanks to my family and friends for your love, support and belief in me and in a hamster named Rocco. I'm lucky to be part of a gang like this one.

ABOUT THE AUTHOR

Angela Robb lives in Stirlingshire, Scotland, and likes nothing better than getting thoroughly lost in the landscape. She studied in Glasgow and Edinburgh and still spends plenty of time in both, soaking up ideas for settings and stories. Small furry pets are, she has discovered, another source of inspiration. *Hamster Gangster* is her first novel.